Starting Over

A Hopes Crest Romance

Book 1

Laura Hayes

Chapter One

Kayla Brady looked up at the old wooden cross as she leaned against the kitchen sink, closed her eyes and lifted up a frantic prayer. "Lord, grant me patience," she whispered. Her temper, which at this moment was as red as her hair, was close to exploding, and she needed to calm down or she would completely lose it.

"Mom," Samantha, Kayla's fourteen-year-old daughter, begged in a tone that sounded shockingly close to a toddler's whine, "It's not that big of a deal. Come on, just let me go. I'm going to look like a nerd if I tell them I can't go with them."

Kayla forced herself to pivot slowly rather than spin out of control and start screaming at her daughter. When she completed the turn and looked at Sam, she felt a twinge of happiness mixed with sadness wash over her. Though Sam had Kayla's temper, her dark hair and eyes were a gift passed down from her father. As was her stubbornness.

"Samantha Jo," Kayla said as she tried to keep her voice under control, "this is not turning into another argument. We've been down this road before. You are not going to Denver with those girls. Now, this discussion is over; I need to get to work and you need to get to school." She grabbed her purse and the truck keys off the counter to emphasize her point.

Sam stood defiantly with her arms crossed over her chest, and the look she gave Kayla was full of rage. "Dad would've let me go," she mumbled with a scowl, and Kayla thought her heart would break into a million pieces.

1

"Don't you dare…" Kayla started to say through clenched teeth, but Sam stomped her foot, turned and headed outside before Kayla could finish her sentence. Whispering another silent prayer, Kayla turned off the kitchen light and headed out to the truck.

It was a typical early May morning with the sun already bright in the sky promising another warm Colorado spring day. She and Sam lived in a large home consisting of five bedrooms that sat on just over twenty acres, more than enough space to house a family of two. However, the way she and Sam had been arguing lately, the house was not big enough to keep them out of each other's hair.

She took a deep breath, allowed the cool mountain air to fill her lungs, and then slowly let it out. There was no way her daughter would be allowed to believe she held the reins in this house, but sometimes Kayla wished she could just hand them over—it would just be so much easier in the short run. But no. Kayla had to look to the long-term, and that meant standing her ground.

"Unlock it already," Sam snapped as she waited beside the passenger's side door.

The short-lived calming feeling dissipated and Kayla debated whether it was worth going to jail for beating one's daughter. But she had to choose her battles, and the girl's attitude wasn't the battle that was the most important at the moment. Using the key fob, she unlocked the door, and Sam hurled herself into the truck as if to show her mother how angry she was.

Kayla looked down at her hand, the diamond on her wedding band catching a glint of the sun. "Brandon, I wish you were here," she whispered, then bit at her lip to stop the tears that threatened to fall. Shaking her head, she got into the truck and glanced over at Sam, who was busy typing away on her phone. Typical. The truck came to life and Kayla sat back against the seat. "Sam, we need to talk."

Sam said nothing and Kayla looked at the clock on the dash. They would be late again if they didn't get going right now. She sighed and reversed the truck out onto the dirt road and then drove toward town. "Hello. Earth to Sam."

Sam mumbled something Kayla could not hear and put her phone in her purse. Then she turned toward Kayla. Though Sam was only fourteen, Kayla could not believe how much she had grown. She was looking older every day, and the realization that she would soon no longer be a girl but a young woman hit Kayla.

"Well?" Sam asked in her annoyed teenage tone that grated on Kayla's nerves. "What did you want to talk about?" How Kayla wished for the time when her only daughter enjoyed her company and showed her a decent amount of respect. Yet, there was a lot of things Kayla missed about the past.

"Your attitude, young lady. Contrary to what you might think, I'm not the meanest mom in town." Kayla glanced in her rear-view mirror and watched the dirt clouds the tires kicked up behind them, which mirrored the path she and her daughter were on—cloudy and no end in sight.

"I feel like those Amish kids on TV," Sam complained. "You don't let me go anywhere, and it's going to be embarrassing that I can't go this weekend." She turned to her mother with a pleading look. "Do you have any idea how it feels to be the laughingstock of the whole school?" Kayla went to respond, but Sam continued talking. "No, you don't, because you were the top cheerleader and everyone loved you. It's hard for me to make friends." She seemed to have run out of steam by the time she finished her rant, and Kayla reached over to take her daughter's hand in her own and gave it a gentle squeeze. Sam was beautiful, had a great personality and had no problems making friends.

"Honey, you have plenty of friends. I think you're so focused on impressing these older girls, you're forgetting about all the other ones you have."

"Maybe," Sam mumbled as Kayla took a left and merged onto the highway into town.

"Look, I get it," Kayla said, relieved they were finally talking rather than shouting. "When my parents wouldn't let me do something, I thought it was the end of the world. You start to assume they have no idea what life is like, especially in school. Sound familiar?"

3

Sam gave a single nod and the start of a smile began to form at the corner of her mouth. "And truth be told, since the day you were born, I've been waiting for a time like this."

Sam turned toward her, her brows scrunched. "What do you mean?"

Kayla tried to maintain a serious face. "To tell you no about going out with your friends. It's what mothers live for. I'm going to leave work early today just so I can go celebrate this momentous occasion." She gave Sam a wink, and then it happened. Sam let out a laugh.

"Alright, I get it," Sam finally conceded. "And, hey," —a tear rolled down her cheek— "I'm sorry what I said about Dad. Forgive me?"

Kayla nodded as she wiped at her own eye. "Forgiven. Now, do you need a ride after school today?"

"I will," Sam replied, her manner returned to the person she truly was. "I'm going to hang out with Emma, so we'll head over to the diner later. Do you mind if she comes over and stays the night tonight?"

"That's fine," Kayla said as she pulled up in front of the school behind a long line of other cars. "I love you."

Hopes Crest Junior/Senior High School had not changed since Kayla had attended eighteen years earlier. The front entrance had a long covered corridor that led to two sets of double doors where students waved to one another as they made their way to their first classes. Benches sat on either side between the brick columns, and Kayla recognized the principal, Linda Miller, as she urged reluctant students into the building.

The woman had not changed since Kayla had attended school with her back in the day. Teenage faces peered from the large windows which spanned the single-story building on either side of the entrance, more than likely hunting for friends who had not yet arrived. The building would not win any glamorous awards, but it was welcoming and accepting.

"Love you, mom," Sam said as she leaned over to give her mother a kiss. At least she had not gotten too old to be embarrassed to do that, for which Kayla was immensely pleased. "See you later."

"Love you too." Kayla smiled as Sam got out of the truck and closed the door behind her. Her smile widened when Sam turned and gave her a wave.

Kayla waved back and then let out a relieved sigh as she said another silent prayer thanking God that she had managed to get through another morning with a teenage daughter. Feeling better, she pulled out and headed to work.

***

A Taste of Heaven Diner was located at the end of a line of various shops and offices along Elm Street, the main business area of Hopes Crest. It boasted a full menu for breakfast, lunch, and dinner and had been a town favorite for many years. Kayla, along with her husband Brandon, had purchased the diner from Mildred Craft, the previous owner, five years earlier, and the plan had been that Kayla run the business until Brandon returned from the service. However, that plan had not panned out, and Kayla was left to carry it out on her own. However, God had not let her down. Most days, like today, plenty of customers frequented the diner to enjoy everything from fresh pancakes for breakfast to steak and baked potatoes for dinner.

Kayla pulled up in front of the building and smiled. *How quickly plans can change*, she thought before she opened the truck door and got out. As she walked inside, she greeted several locals by name. The diner was square with booths along each wall and two rows of small tables running down the middle. Breakfast was always the busiest time, but with the tourist season soon approaching, it would stay busy all day through dinner.

The kitchen was in what Carl, the cook, considered 'organized chaos'. "Hey, Miss Kayla," he said as she came through the side door. "How're you doing today?"

"I'm doing well," she replied. Carl insisted on calling her 'Miss Kayla' even though she was close to the same age as him and it always amused her to no end. "Not a father yet?"

"No, ma'am," he said with a goofy grin. "But I think Mindy's about to burst. Hey, did you find my replacement yet?"

Kayla shook her head. "I haven't, but I do have an interview today around two. I'll let you know how that goes." She had been surprised when he had asked for time off once the baby was born but could not deny that it was a sweet gesture on his part. Times sure had changed since she had Sam, that was for sure.

Carl gave her a smile. "Sounds good." He placed a plate of chicken fried steak and eggs on the shelf and tapped a small bell. "Order up!" he called out.

Susan, one of the waitresses and Kayla's best friend, walked up and grabbed the plate. "About time you showed up," she teased. "Always walking in like you own the place." She shot Kayla a wink.

"Love you, too," Kayla said with a laugh and then headed back into her tiny office. It only had enough room for a shelf against the wall to serve as her desk, a chair, a four-drawer filing cabinet and a small bookshelf.

A small picture sat on her desk, taken just over four years earlier. It showed her, Brandon, and Sam in front of one of the Seven Falls in Colorado Springs, and the memory brought tears to her eyes. It was the last photo they had taken as a family.

Kayla shook her head to clear the thoughts from her mind, used the mouse on her computer, and printed off the resume of the man who was coming in today to interview as Carl's replacement. She was sad to see Carl go, he was a great cook, very reliable and trustworthy, but she could understand that he wanted time with his wife and their new baby.

She studied the resume. James Cole, 37. Worked in a diner in Denver for the last four years. Kayla had already called in for the reference and the manager had given James nothing but praise. She would more than likely hire him as long as the interview went well. The job had been posted around town for the last two weeks and so far not a single person had shown interest, which surprised Kayla; there was always someone looking for work in Hopes Crest.

"Hey, girlfriend, how are you?" Susan asked as she leaned against the door jamb.

Kayla twisted in the chair and smiled. She and Susan had been best friends since grade school and time had not made them less so. Sure, they had their issues, as any friends did, but they cared enough for each other to always talk things through, regardless of what was going on. Each had been a great support to the other, and Kayla knew Susan had been specifically placed in her life by God Himself.

"I'm good," Kayla replied, giving Susan a big hug. "I had some problems with Sam this morning, but by the time I dropped her off, we had worked it out."

"The teenage years," Susan said with a grimace. "I feel sorry for you." She leaned against the door. "I was going to ask; do you have any plans tonight?"

"No," Kayla replied. "Sam may have Emma over, so I need to be there. Why? What's up?"

"Oh, nothing planned," Susan said. "I just wanted to know if you wanted some company."

Kayla smiled. "Sure, sounds good." She always enjoyed spending time with Susan, and having another adult in the house would make her feel as if she had backup. Not that she really ever had problems with the girls when they were over, but she wasn't about ready to pass up the extra eyes and ears.

"Order up!" Carl shouted from the kitchen, making both Kayla and Susan turn.

"Alright, I better get back," Susan said and then hurried out of office.

Kayla smiled, returned to her desk, and began to go through the paperwork for the day. Though it had started out rough, Kayla had a feeling things were only going to get better.

Chapter Two

T he last customer left only a few minutes ago, and Kayla sat in a booth and stared out onto Elm Street. It was the inevitable slow period between lunch and dinner, and they would be lucky if even one customer came in.

However, it gave them time to clean up after lunch and prep for the dinner rush. Susan was rolling silverware and Betty was cleaning the soda machine while Carl was making sure everything in the kitchen was up to his high standards.

Kayla should have been working on the books in her office, but she found her mind going back to the day she and Brandon purchased the diner. It had been a spring morning and they were both over the moon to be starting this new chapter in their lives.

Susan walked up to Kayla with her tub of silverware and the cloth napkins they used for dinner and sat across from her. "Are you doing okay?" she asked, breaking Kayla from her thoughts.

Kayla turned and gave her a nod. "Yeah, I'm fine. I was just thinking is all."

Susan placed a hand over hers. "Well, tonight we're going to have a glass of wine and get all that junk that's been bothering you out and dealt with," she said.

This made Kayla laugh. "I never said I was bottling anything up."

"You don't have to," Susan replied. "I've known you for way too long to not know when something's troubling you."

The loud rumble of a motorcycle made them turn to look out the window, and Susan's jaw dropped. "Oh, my!" she said appreciatively as a man in a tank top that showed a defined torso and well-muscled arms that were covered in tattoos flicked out the kickstand and dismounted.

He reached into a side bag and pulled out a short-sleeved, button-up shirt and put it on as he glanced around the square with what appeared to be great interest.

"Kayla!" Susan said breathlessly, "I bet that's the guy for the interview."

Kayla suddenly felt light-headed and found it hard to speak. Why, she did not know, but the feeling was almost overwhelming.

"Whatever you do," Betty, who had walked up to see what was going on, said, "please hire him. That's some eye candy right there."

"Betty!" Kayla said with a gasp. "You shouldn't say things like that." To be honest, Betty was right; he was a very nice-looking man, but that did not mean they needed to stand around making comments and ogling at him like he was some sort of one-man show.

As the man walked past the large window, Kayla's eyes met his through the glass. They were a deep brown, much like his hair, and Kayla's breathlessness returned. "Okay, you two, look busy," she ordered as she slid out of the booth. "No more gawking."

The door opened and the man walked in. Kayla found herself unable to move as the man approached her, as if some strange arctic storm had blown through and frozen her into place. He was at least four inches taller than her, and she was not all that short. He brushed back a wave of brown hair that had fallen over his face and Kayla found herself reminded of the men who graced the covers of the romance novels she had seen when she was a teenager.

For a moment, her mind wandered. She could picture him picking her up and placing her on his motorcycle—in the novels it was always a horse—and they would ride out into the mountains, her hair flowing behind her as she held onto his biceps for support. They could have a picnic lunch on a small patch of grass while a large aspen tree provided shade from the sun. He would pick a flower for her and present it to her...

"Hi," the man said and Kayla almost jumped. "I'm James. I'm here to speak to Kayla."

Kayla swallowed hard, trying to bring moisture back to her suddenly dry throat. What in the world was wrong with her?

"Hi," she said, then felt her cheeks go red when she realized that she was staring at his arms. She forced herself to look back up at his face, but even that was distracting. Whatever her issue was, she needed to get it under control, and fast. She offered him her hand. "I'm Kayla," she said, forcing a confidence she did not feel into her voice. "You must be James." She cringed as he let out a small laugh.

He grabbed her hand and shook it. "Yes, I'm James," he said in his voice amused.

A woozy feeling came over her. Though his hand was calloused, it was gentle, yet firm, and she found herself pulling her hand away carefully but quickly, as if he were a snake that might bite her. "Let's have a seat," she said. "Pick wherever you want to sit. I don't care." Her cheeks burned even hotter. Why was she acting like a high school girl? She glanced over his shoulder at Susan who gave her a thumbs up sign and then made a kissing face. Kayla wanted to march right over to the woman and give her a good smack.

"This booth works," James said before walking over and taking a seat.

Kayla glanced back at Susan, whose hands were clasped against her chest as she batted her eyelashes. Shooing her away with a silent wave of her hand, Kayla walked over to the booth and sat down to face James. "So, James, tell me about yourself."

"Let's see," he replied. "I'm thirty-seven. I just moved here three days ago and am living in the trailer park a few blocks over." He pointed out the window toward Mason Street. "I have restaurant experience and can work the line, wait tables, paint the walls. Whatever you need, I can do it."

"That's wonderful." Kayla let out a sigh. He seemed so perfect.

"Are you the manager?"

"Oh, sorry. I'm the owner. This is my place. I own it." Kayla bit at her lip. Feeling even sillier than she had when he had first entered, she looked out the window. "So, a motorcycle, huh?"

"Yes," he replied with a wide smile. "I've had it for a few years. I usually take my truck out, but it was too nice of a day not go for a ride on it."

"I agree," Kayla said as she stared at the machine. "I love motorcycles." For a moment she thought back to what it would be like to ride on the motorcycle with him. The wind blowing through her hair as she wrapped her arms around his waist. Maybe they would pull off the side of the road and watch the sun set together.

"Oh, that's cool," James said with a distinct interest. "What kind of bike do you have?"

Kayla bit at her lip. She felt like climbing under the table, not this one, of course, but maybe the one in the back corner...of the newspaper office across the street. "Well, I don't own one, not yet. I mean, I had thought about buying one." Of course, she had thought about it - for about a minute when she was eighteen and never gave it a second thought since, so it wasn't technically a lie.

"Oh, okay. So, do you ride often?" he asked as he leaned back in the booth.

"No," she managed to mumble.

"Well, I'd be happy to take you out sometime on mine," he said. Then it was his turn to grimace. "I mean, was that okay to offer? Sorry."

"Oh, no. I would love to," she said, then she shook her head. She was supposed to be interviewing him for a job, not a date. She looked down at the ring on her finger. Brandon had passed away four years ago, and though she had been praying lately for God to send someone into her life, a wave of guilt washed over her. She was lonely and desperately wanted a man in her life, but she could not stop the fear that tried to overtake her. Was she being unfaithful even though her husband was gone? Pastor Dave had said it was perfectly fine for her to start dating and even remarry one day.

At that moment, her heart and mind began an inner battle, and she was not sure which one was going to win.

***

James Cole let out a small sigh as he sat in the booth for his interview. The day had started out perfectly. He had driven out to Lake Hope, which was located two miles from his house, and spent an hour there by the shore praying and thanking God for all He had given him—the opportunity to move to Hopes Crest, the finances in which to do so, and finally, the job opening. He had also prayed, as he often did, for God to send him someone, someone he could share his life with.

When James had seen Kayla, the woman interviewing him now, he thought that maybe she was that woman. Her laugh, her smile, she was definitely someone he would not mind spending time with, maybe even dating. It was obvious she was a bit nervous around him; she fumbled her words and her cheeks had gone red more than once. But then he inwardly scolded himself for offering the motorcycle ride. Not so much for the offer itself, but now, as she looked down at her hand, he saw the large diamond on the wedding band.

Though she seemed like a nice woman, he had no interest in getting involved with a married woman. It was a shame because he had hoped that maybe she was the one. But apparently God had other plans.

Kayla looked back up and a timid smile came across her face. "I guess I could go sometime," she said.

James could see the struggle on her face and the worry in her eyes, and he hoped he could get out of the situation without it costing him a job. "You know, I just remembered my insurance doesn't cover passengers," he said. It was a lie and he hated having to do it, but this woman's marriage was far more important.

"Oh, I see," she said with clear disappointment.

He smiled as he clasped his hands on the table in front of him. It was best if he moved the conversation back to the job at hand. That was what he was here for, not for picking up women. "So, about this job. The website said morning shift?"

The question seemed to do the trick, and it was like she snapped out of a haze. Her smile came back, and she gave a single nod. "That's right," she replied, her tone back to business. "Six in the morning until two.

Deborah comes in just before that; she's the night cook." She stood. "Come on, I'll show you around."

James slid out of the booth and followed Kayla up to a small workstation. He smiled at the two waitresses as Kayla introduced them.

"This is Susan," she said, indicating a woman who was around Kayla's age with long blond hair, "and Betty." The younger woman pushed a strand of her short dark hair back behind an ear and gave him a wide smile.

"Nice to meet you, ladies," he said, shaking each of their hands. Both women grinned and then returned to their duties. He followed Kayla through a swinging door into the kitchen.

A blond man with a red apron walked up to them and put out his hand. "You must be James," he said pleasantly. "I'm Carl." He raised an eyebrow. "So, did you get hired?"

James glanced over at Kayla. "I don't know," he said. He hoped that canceling the motorcycle ride did not put him in danger of not getting the job.

"We're still discussing it," Kayla replied. "But if you're hired, Carl here will help you train." She started down a short hallway and James figured he probably was supposed to follow her. They stopped at what looked like a small office and Kayla opened a metal folding chair and set it inside the doorway just before taking a seat in an office chair. "Have a seat."

James looked around the tiny room. It was well-organized and clean, much like its owner. His eyes fell on a photo in a silver picture frame that sat on the desk. Kayla, a man in a military uniform who had to be her husband, and a young girl no older than ten smiled back at him.

"We're closed Sundays and Mondays," Kayla said as she sifted through one of the lower drawers in the filing cabinet. "I pay ten an hour, meals are on the house. If you can show up on time and do a good job, I would like to welcome you to our family."

James stared at her for a second as he tried to soak in the news. Then he smiled and said a silent prayer of thanks.

He had secured a home and now a new job. God truly was good. "Thank you. I accept," he said.

"Good. So, what brought you out here to Hopes Crest?" She placed a paper clip on several sheets of paper as she spoke. She certainly was a multitasker.

"I lived in Denver for so long, I was itching to get moving. You know, try somewhere else. Well, a guy I used to work with mentioned this place. He said he vacationed out here for a day on his way heading out of the state and really liked how quiet it was. Long story short, I went online, looked the place up and started making plans." He leaned back in his chair. "I can't believe that, with all the years I've lived in Colorado, I never came up this way."

"That's great," Kayla said and then handed him the papers. "Paperwork for taxes and what not. I don't require uniforms, so a shirt and jeans are fine. I usually show up before nine, but Susan is here every morning to open."

James took the packet and stood up. "I want to thank you for this opportunity," he said, extending his hand to her. "It means a lot."

Kayla rose, took his hand and gave James a firm handshake. "I know it wasn't a conventional interview," she said with a wide smile, "but it's how I like to do things. Like I said, we're a family here, and it's more than just words. If you need anything, just ask."

James thanked her again and then walked through the door. He stopped and took a quick glance over his shoulder. Kayla sat with her elbows on the desk and was playing with her wedding band again. It brought sadness to his heart.

Lord, help this woman with her struggles, he prayed.

He headed back through the kitchen and then outside. The sun was shining brightly and its warm rays felt great. The Lord looked after His own, and though James had been through some hard times in life, God had always lifted him up, even when it felt like the last minute. And now he was in a new town with a new home and a new job. Life was great and he looked forward to a fresh chapter in his life.

Chapter Three

The doorbell rang and Kayla dug into her purse and pulled out her wallet. Sam and Emma waited patiently for her to pull out some cash to pay the pizza delivery boy, and Kayla laughed when Sam's smile grew when Kayla gave her the money.

"Do you want me to help you girls get the food?" she asked with as much innocence as she could muster.

Both girls' jaws dropped in horror. "Mom!" Sam said in a shocked tone. "No way!"

Kayla laughed as the girls rushed to the front door. Kyle, the delivery boy, was, as the girls put it, 'the hottest guy in town'. Kayla smiled as she returned her wallet to her purse and set the purse back on the table. She went to the kitchen and grabbed a stack of plates, napkins, and several cans of Coke.

"I hope you don't mind," Sam said as she came back into the kitchen with two pizza boxes in her arms, "I tipped him five bucks." Kayla smiled, a shake to her head.

"Sure, that's fine," Kayla replied. She probably would have done the same anyway. "Did you manage to say hi to him without stuttering?"

Emma put her arm around Sam and smiled proudly. "To be honest, Kayla, she did. I was impressed," she teased.

Sam went a bright shade of red and flicked a light slap on her friend's arm.

They began serving up the food and then a thought struck Kayla. Sam's reaction to Kyle was very much like Kayla's reaction earlier to James. Then another thought hit her as she opened up one of the Cokes;

she had openly flirted with a new employee. Not only did it not set a good example for her other employees, especially how Susan and Betty had acted when they saw James outside, but Kayla's actions might have made James himself uncomfortable. How could she have been so foolish? It just wasn't like her to be so forward.

She pushed the thoughts out of her head. What was done was done. All she could do now was learn from it and move on.

"So, what are you two girls up to this evening?" she asked in an attempt to bring herself back to the present.

Sam set her pizza down and, without looking at Kayla, said, "Well, first we're going to eat. Then we'll take the truck out on the town. We're supposed to meet some older guys we met online and then go get tattoos together." She flashed Kayla a smile.

Kayla pointed her finger at her daughter. "Watch it," she said. "I told you before, you can only meet strangers online on a Saturday night, never a Friday night."

"Darn," Sam said, snapping her fingers as if just remembering the crazy rule.

Emma's eyes went wide. She and Sam had only been friends less than a year and apparently still hadn't caught on to their sense of humor just yet.

"I'm kidding and so is Sam," Kayla assured Emma. She took a seat on one of the stools at the counter. "How are you liking Hopes Crest so far?"

"I like it," Emma replied. Then she let out a sigh. "But to be honest, I miss my dad back in Denver."

Kayla's heart went out to her. From what she had heard, Emma's parents went through a nasty divorce and it was apparent Emma had been caught in the middle. "I'm sorry, honey," she said, reaching over and giving the girl's hand a pat. "Do you get to see him at all?"

Emma nodded. "I'm going to visit him for a few weeks this summer. But he has a new girlfriend and she takes up all of his time." She rolled her eyes at this.

Kayla glanced at Sam who gave her a sad nod.

"Well, you are more than welcome here anytime you like," Kayla offered. "I know Sam loves having you over, and I think you're pretty cool." Kayla received a groan from Sam. "What?"

"Cool?" Sam said. "No one ever wants to hear from you that they're cool. It's like, weird."

"I will have you know," Kayla said as she wiped her fingers on a napkin, "I was considered very cool in school." She grabbed another slice of pizza. "As a matter of fact..." The doorbell rang and she let out a sigh. "Well, I'll have to tell you about that some other time. Susan and I will be out back if you need me."

Sam nodded and the two girls each grabbed another slice of pizza and headed upstairs to Sam's room as Kayla went to open the door.

Susan stood there with a bottle of wine in her hand and a mischievous smile on her face. "You have got to tell me about Mr. Hunk," she said, walking right past Kayla.

Kayla laughed as they headed into the kitchen, and Susan went straight to a cabinet and pulled out two wine glasses. "So? What about him?"

Kayla glanced toward the stairs and then put a finger to her lips. Susan nodded as Kayla motioned at the pizza.

"Are you hungry?" Kayla asked as if Susan had not said anything. "There's plenty to go around."

"No thanks. I ate a salad just before I came over. Come on, let's go out back."

Kayla smiled. Susan was always making suggestions and asking questions, and Kayla knew a lot of questions were coming her way. They headed out the French doors to the patio where they had an unobstructed view of both the private lake she shared and the mountain range behind it. A path snaked its way down a small incline right down to a small beach at the edge of the lake.

As it was, the house was far too large for three people, but she and Brandon had purchased the home in anticipation of adding more family members. That is until he passed away. Although the house was now that much bigger for two people, Kayla could not get herself to sell it and buy something smaller. It was simply too beautiful to leave.

Susan poured them each a glass of wine and handed one to Kayla. "Well, take it," she said. "I'm not going to force you."

Kayla thanked her and they both sat side by side on a padded rocking bench. She took a sip of the wine, loving the fruit flavor as it rolled down her throat.

"So, what's up with the hunk?" Susan asked. "You went quiet on me earlier."

"I hired him, of course," Kayla replied, "but not because of his looks."

Susan snorted. "Sure, you didn't," she teased. "Well, what about him? I mean, is he more than just looks?"

"Yes," Kayla said. "He seems really nice and has a friendly smile. I think he's going to make a great addition to our work family."

Susan turned toward Kayla, who recognized the woman's serious stance. "How did it feel flirting with him?" she asked.

Kayla bit at her lip, her heart pulling in every direction imaginable. "I don't know," she replied. "It felt good at first, but then I felt, I don't know…guilty." She heaved a heavy sigh. "I keep thinking that it's like I'm cheating on Brandon. But then I feel like he would want me to move on." She stared off over the lake. "I don't know, I'm just confused." A flock of birds flew past them and soon disappeared into the horizon.

"I knew Brandon as long as you did," Susan said as she took Kayla's hand in hers. "That man wanted you to be happy. I'm not just saying this because you're my best friend; I think he would be fine with you moving on. In fact, I think he would encourage it."

Kayla nodded. She knew Susan was right; Brandon would want that. The question was, did she?

"Let me ask you this," Susan added. "Have you prayed about it?"

Kayla took another sip of her wine before replying. "That's the thing. I've been praying, sharing with the Lord how lonely I've been feeling. And then it's like he places this man in front of me who I'm immediately attracted to. I don't know if he's even a believer, but there's a glow around him. Something good about him. But then, well, it went downhill pretty quickly."

"What do you mean?" Susan asked.

Kayla moved her hair back over her shoulder and replayed the motorcycle ride offer fiasco in her head. How she wished she could go back in time and stop it from happening, but that would never happen, so she was stuck with what she had said.

"I kind of lied to him about liking motorcycles, so he offered me a chance to go for a ride with him. Then a minute later, he made some excuse about not having insurance for a passenger." She shook her head. "It was like it was all building up, then boom! it all fell flat." Kayla let out a sigh of frustration and set her wine glass on the side table. "What do you think? Did I scare him off?"

Susan smiled and took Kayla's hand in her own. "I think this might have caused a problem," she said, glancing down to Kayla's hand.

Kayla looked down at her wedding band. "I know, I told you I was feeling guilty," Kayla said, not sure what Susan was getting at.

"No, honey, I think your new employee saw it and then backed off. If that's the case, you have a good man at the diner and your decision to hire him was right."

Kayla's eyes went wide as she recalled the guilt she felt earlier during the interview. Now it was like she could see herself from outside the situation and watched as she played with the ring while sitting in the booth. "Oh, wow! Poor guy. He must think I'm pretty horrible."

"I know I sure do," Susan teased and they both laughed.

Kayla leaned over and gave her friend a hug and then wiped a tear from her eye. "You know, I'm going to pray later tonight, really seek God's wisdom in this situation."

"Good," Susan said as she stood, making the bench lurch back a bit. "Now, I'm going to get me a slice of pizza. It looked too good to pass up." She headed back inside the house leaving Kayla alone.

Looking back over the mountain range, Kayla felt herself smile. Prayer was the one thing that had helped her with the loss of Brandon, and she was looking forward to hearing from God tonight.

***

It was past midnight, and Susan had already left and the girls were in Sam's room, the indistinct muffle of voices on the TV sounding behind the closed door. Kayla had just said goodnight to the girls and had headed back to her own room. Quickly changing into her pajamas, she went to the foot of her bed and knelt in prayer. She had learned a long time ago that God wanted to hear what was on a person's heart. Long drawn out prayers that sounded like they came from Fifteenth-Century England were not needed. But honesty was.

"Lord, it's been really tough lately and I need your help," Kayla began her prayer. For the next ten minutes she prayed not only for her situation, but for Sam as well. Their relationship had its ups and downs and she needed help there as much as she did in her personal life. She finished off her prayers with requests for peace for Emma and her family. "Amen," she said in conclusion and she stood up and walked over to a photo of her and Brandon. Taken on their honeymoon in Hawaii, it seemed like it was a lifetime ago when they were both eighteen struggling with the nervousness and fear of him leaving to join the Marines.

"I've missed you every day, Brandon," she whispered as tears ran unchecked down her face. She did not try to stop them, for tears led to healing. "But I'm ready to move on. I've been so lonely since you left us. I don't know if this new man is the one for me or not, but whoever the Lord puts in my path, I know he will be a good man who will look after Sam and me, just like you did." She looked down at her wedding band and smiled before slipping it off her finger. "I love you, Brandon. I always have and I always will." She opened the top drawer of the dresser, placed the ring inside and felt an odd sense of relief when she closed the drawer again. There was no guilt but rather a sense of peace.

Glancing over, she looked at the photos of Sam beginning from when she was an infant to one taken just this past Christmas. Not only did Kayla need a man in her life for herself, but for Sam, too. A man to go fishing with her or just to be a father figure. Whether it was James or someone else, Kayla did not know. But one thing she did know, she was now ready for whomever God put in her life.

Chapter Four

S unday morning, Kayla pulled the truck into a space at Hopes Crest Church. It was a nondenominational church with roughly two hundred members, and she had attended it since she was a kid. It had always been a place of solace and encouragement, a place she could always count on when times were troubled. Where she had always loved going. However, her daughter had taken to complaining about it.

"Sundays are meant for sleeping in," Sam groaned as Kayla turned the truck off. "I mean, I like going sometimes, but every Sunday is a drag."

Kayla let out a sigh and smoothed out her purple dress. Turning to her daughter, she wondered why the girl's rebellion had been getting worse over the last year. No doubt some of it was the fact that she was a teenager, but something else was bothering her, something Kayla had yet to figure out or get Sam to admit.

"Honey, you used to love going," Kayla said. "Why don't you anymore?"

Sam shrugged in a moody manner and then opened the door. All Kayla could do was stare after her as she slammed the door shut. Whatever was bothering Sam was only getting worse, and Kayla was beside herself with worry. She once again sent up a silent prayer for patience as she got out of the truck and walked around to where Sam was waiting.

Summer had come early this year, creating high temperatures that were a rarity for May. One of the joys of living in the mountains was that it rarely got above eighty in the summer, and with the darker clouds, she doubted it would be above seventy-five today. She was glad they did not live in the foothills where the temperature was supposed to reach the mid-nineties.

Kayla put her arm around her daughter's shoulders, her sleeveless black dress cut in the same style as the one Kayla wore. "You look pretty," she said as they headed toward the door.

"Thanks," Sam muttered as they headed up the steps, though she did not sound as appreciative of Kayla's compliment as her comment was meant to be.

The usher handed Kayla a pamphlet and Kayla thanked him before moving into the foyer. She waved at a few familiar faces and then moved through the open double doors into the nave where rows of pews sat facing the front. Services would be starting in just a few minutes and already the place was packed. Directly in front of them was the chancel with the pulpit in the center at the top of two steps. A small band was set up to the left of the pulpit and risers where the choir stood sat to the right. However, the most prominent object at the front of the church was the large wooden cross that rested on the back wall.

Kayla and Sam walked down the aisle toward their usual seats. It was funny how, every Sunday, each person who attended the church had his or her specific spot in which to sit, and it rarely deviated. As a matter of fact, if anyone entered the nave and saw their seat taken, it was not uncommon to see a brief glint of annoyance on the face of whomever usually had that seat. Unless the usurper was new, then they were forgiven much more quickly than someone who regularly attended.

"Hey, Kayla, Sam, how are you?"

Kayla turned and smiled at Maria, the pastor's wife, a beautiful woman who was only a few years older than Kayla with jet black hair and deep brown eyes.

"Good morning," Kayla replied with a hug. "We're well. How are you?"

"Busy as always," Maria said with a laugh. "Hey, look, I needed to ask a huge favor. We have a new member, and I know this is really asking a lot…" Her voice trailed off.

"Name it. We don't mind, do we, Sam?" Kayla said, giving her daughter a gentle elbow.

"No. Not at all." She did not sound convincing, but at least she had responded.

"Well, Dolores is out of town and he needs someone to sit with. Would you mind making him feel at home?" Dolores Van Schneider was about seventy years old and tough as leather. She was old-school and had always had an air of arrogance about her, but she had always been a pillar in the community, so everyone simply allowed her whatever rants she felt needed to be voiced and then moved on with their lives. However, Kayla would wish it on no one to sit next to the woman, even if she were here, and would do what she could to help the poor soul.

"Of course," Kayla replied with a happy smile. "That won't be a problem."

Maria turned toward the doors and smiled. "James, over here!" she said with a wave of her hand.

Kayla thought her heart would burst from her chest as she turned and watched her newest employee amble toward them. Not only was he dressed in dark jeans, but the short-sleeved button-up shirt he wore did nothing to conceal his well-defined arms.

"Wow, mom!" Sam whispered. "Check that dude out. He looks like some sort of pro wrestler or something." Kayla could not have said it better.

"Hey, Kayla," James said as he stuck out his hand. "Wow, it's great to see you."

"Oh, you two know each other?" Maria asked.

Kayla nodded as she shook James's hand, wondering at the giddy feeling that had washed over her. She had prayed last night for direction and seeing James here this morning could not be taken as anything more than an answer to those prayers.

"We do," James replied before Kayla could find her voice. "Kayla here was kind enough to hire me at the diner as a morning cook. I start Tuesday."

Maria smiled. "That's great," she said. Then she looked over toward the far doors. "Sorry, I really need to talk to Dave. James, if you have any questions, Kayla will be able to help you."

"Thanks," James replied, and then Maria walked off.

"Mom," Sam whispered, "stop staring at him and introduce me."

Kayla felt as if a furnace had been set right next to her. "Oh, right," she said. "Yes. James, this is my daughter Sam."

James smiled and shook Sam's hand. "Nice to meet you."

"Yeah, you, too," Sam replied.

"This is great, you two attend this church," James said. Then he glanced around when the choir began to sing. "Should we grab a seat?"

"Good idea," Kayla replied. "Follow me." She led him and Sam to their usual seats and had to stifle a laugh when she saw Susan flash her a thumbs-up sign. As if she was not four shades of red already! "This is where we usually sit," Kayla said when they got to the third row.

James extended his hand. "Ladies," he said politely.

Kayla ushered Sam in first and then sat beside her. She glanced up at James and was shocked to see he had a frown on his face.

"Do you mind scooting down one more?" he asked.

Kayla shrugged, asked Sam to move down before she took Sam's now vacant seat, and was shocked when James sat on the end leaving the seat between him and Kayla empty.

"You're welcome to sit next to me," Kayla said with a laugh. "I may look mean, but I really don't bite."

James gave her a stern look. "I think I should save that for your husband," he said firmly.

Kayla went to correct him but the band had begun a lively song and it was difficult to hear over the noise of the drums. She resigned herself to explain to him later as the congregation stood at the direction of the pastor.

During the songs, she kept glancing over at James, and try as she might, she could not keep herself from smiling. Not that church did not make her smile anyway, but being so close to such a handsome man who was also such a gentleman brought on a sense of joy. He was single, at least as far as she knew, which was great, but he was in church, and that made it all the better.

The final song came to a close and Pastor Dave took his place behind the pulpit. His dark brown hair had patches of gray, and at forty, he wore that gray proudly.

"The last time we had this many in attendance," he was saying, "was when we promised everyone pizza." The congregation laughed. "But in all seriousness, it's good to see everyone. Now, sit down and give your legs a rest." This brought on more laughter as people sat back down.

Kayla glanced over at Sam, who was on her cell phone. She gave her daughter a quick tap on her knee and put her hand out. Sam let out a frustrated sigh and reluctantly placed the phone in Kayla's hand, which Kayla put in her own purse.

"You'll get it back after church," Kayla whispered.

Sam glared at her mother. "I can put it away," she snapped back.

"Well, how about this?" Kayla said as she smoothed the irritation from her face. "I'll just keep it for the next two days and we'll call it good."

The look Sam gave should have frozen Kayla in place, but Kayla refused to budge. She had had enough of her daughter's disrespect. One day she would get to the bottom of what her daughter was struggling with, but until then, she had to do what she could to keep the upper hand. Ah, the life of the mother of a teenager.

"We have a new member today that I already had the pleasure of meeting," Pastor Dave was saying, and Kayla pushed the cell phone from her mind. "James, would you mind standing up for us so we can welcome you?"

James stood up and gave a self-conscious wave as people clapped.

"Oh, honey, he is such a hunk," Susan whispered in Kayla's ear from the row behind her.

Kayla turned halfway and whispered, "This is church! Now stop it!" It took everything in her power to not burst out laughing. However, she glanced around and realized that all eyes were on her. Beside her, Sam groaned. Kayla made a mental note to strangle Susan after the service.

James smiled, leaned over and whispered, "The pastor asked about the bake sale?"

Kayla thought she would die from embarrassment right there and then. She cleared her throat and jutted her chin out defiantly. "Sorry," she said as she stood. "Yes. Well, the bake sale for next week is still on after the service. We'll set up as usual in the foyer."

Pastor Dave thanked her as she retook her seat. She turned to James and was glad to see a smile on his face. "Thank you," she whispered.

He nodded and then turned back to look toward the front. When Pastor Dave called for the first prayers of the morning, Kayla sent a prayer thanking God for all He had given her and the things He always revealed to her. She prayed for Sam and for a strengthening of their currently rocky relationship. And finally, she prayed for the possibility of a relationship that continued to reappear in the man named James.

***

Ten minutes after the service finished, most of the congregation had cleared out. However, a dozen or so people stood in small pairs or clusters engaged in conversation. Kayla was one such person speaking with Susan.

"So," Susan was saying in a hushed, but decisive, tone, "not only did you pray for this for the past two nights, God puts him right into the seat next to you. I swear, it's a sign."

Kayla gave a quick nod of agreement. "It sure looks that way," she replied. Then she bit at her bottom lip. "But he didn't want to sit next to me. He thinks I'm still married. I need to clear the air with him about that."

"Yeah, you do," Susan said with a small snort. "Because there's no way you want that hunk of muscles to find someone else."

Kayla shook her head. "You're terrible! Yes, he has lots of muscles, and yes, he's as handsome as anything, but I want to get to know him better first. Personality plays a huge part in it."

Susan raised her hands up in mock defeat. "You got me there," she said. Then she leaned in and whispered, "Can I touch his bicep? Do you mind?"

"You haven't changed one bit since high school," Kayla replied. "I don't care; he's not my boyfriend."

James walked up and Kayla hoped beyond all hopes he had not overheard any of their conversation. "James," Kayla said, "You remember Susan from the diner?"

"I sure do," he replied with a smile. "Good to see you again." He offered her his hand and Susan took it.

"Good to see you, too," Susan replied, and then, much to Kayla's mortification, Susan let out a small laugh and reached out to pat his bicep. When she was finished with what Kayla could only name as 'feeling up' James's arm, she asked, "Did Kayla invite you to lunch today?"

Kayla wondered how quickly she could dig a hole and bury herself in it. Why this woman felt the need to play matchmaker was beyond her.

James, however, had an amused look on his face. "No."

"Oh? Well, I'll let her explain it to you. I'll be there, as well." She shot Kayla a wide smile. "I'll go get Sam for you."

Before Kayla could even thank her—although she was not sure if thanking the woman was really what Kayla wanted to do at that moment—Susan was gone, leaving Kayla and James staring after her.

Kayla's mind swirled as she realized she needed to clear the air about her marriage before she even broached the subject of inviting him over for lunch. Otherwise, even if Susan promised to be there, she doubted he would accept.

"Okay, first off, I need to explain something to you." She glanced around. There were still a couple of people in the nave and though everyone knew about Brandon, Kayla felt better about discussing things in private. "Do you mind if we step outside?"

He hesitated but finally agreed, and they found themselves beside Kayla's truck.

"Look," he said before she could speak, "I don't want to be rude or anything, and I really appreciate your kindness in asking me to lunch, but I don't think it's appropriate for me to go to lunch with you. You're married and I don't want to give you the wrong impression."

Kayla sighed. He was handsome and a true gentleman. She was over the moon. "Well, that's the thing—I'm not married."

His eyebrows crunched and he raised a single eyebrow. "Not to argue," he said, "but your ring…" he glanced down at her now bare hand and his eyes widened. "Well, I did see one."

"You did," Kayla replied. "Let me explain."

"Please do." He leaned his arm against the truck and gave her an expectant look that only made her nervous. Did he think she was going to lie to him?

"I'll be happy to explain more later, but my husband Brandon passed away four years ago."

"Oh, I see. I am so sorry," he said with a shocked look.

She thanked him and then continued. "So, I…well, it's totally safe for us to eat lunch together. I mean…you're not with anyone, are you?"

He shook his head and let out a heavy breath as if he had been holding it. "No, thankfully, I'm not." His cheeks reddened, and when he smiled, Kayla noticed a cute dimple show up that made her heart swoon. "What I mean to say is I'm single. So, yes, I would love to join you for lunch."

Kayla's heart beat so hard against her chest, she wondered if he could see her chest move from it.

"Hey, mom, are we leaving yet?" Sam asked as she and Susan approached. "I'm hungry."

"Yeah," Kayla replied. Then she turned back to James. "Want to follow us?"

"Sure, I'm in the old black Chevy," he said, pointing at a truck that sat now sat alone one section over.

"All right, see you in a few." Kayla watched him walk away and when she turned, Sam had a scowl on her face. "What?"

"I'm hungry," Sam said in an irritated voice.

Kayla's jaw clenched, as did her fist, but Susan's voice came in a whisper, "She's just a teenager. Mind yourself."

Kayla relaxed her hand and gave Susan a hug. "See you in a few."

Teenager or not, Sam needed her attitude adjusted. How to go about that, however, Kayla had no idea.

Chapter Five

James tapped his fingers on the steering wheel as he followed Kayla's truck off the highway and onto a dirt road just outside of town. He was shocked when he saw her in church today and even more so when he found out she was not married as he had thought she was. It was difficult to fight off the confusion he felt. On one hand, his heart went out to her being a widow. Yet, at the same time, he could not help but feel glad she was not a married woman wanting to fool around on an absent husband.

Now he was curious as to how this lunch should be perceived. Was it a date? On the onset, no; it was an offer for lunch, which was a sign of hospitality, a welcoming to the church, even if it was in her home. It was not as if this was his first invite of this type. Regardless, he reminded himself that, even though Kayla was a beautiful woman and he had been praying for the past few years for God to send him someone with whom he could spend his life, he had to be certain not to mix signals just in case she was not that woman.

The dirt road curved up and James's jaw dropped as the truck crested a large hill and the sun glinted off a large lake with a mountain range behind it. The sight was breathtaking. On either side of the lake sat a dozen mansions nestled in trees atop rolling hills, six on each side, and all of them were massive.

He had to fight off panic as he wondered how he was going to fit in. He hardly had any savings, and the old truck he drove was a sign that he did not have much. However, he smiled as he remembered that he had something money could not buy, a gift far better than anything in the world.

Salvation. That sweet, unconditional gift that was paid for nearly two thousand years ago. Being the recipient of that gift was far more precious and worth more than any material thing, and by the time he pulled the truck up next to Kayla's much newer one, the sense of peace had returned.

Up close, the house was even more imposing. James had grown up in trailer parks and dilapidated apartment buildings, and despite his inner peace, he still hoped that redneck part of him would not suddenly pop out and embarrass him.

"If they offer food you can't pronounce," he counseled himself, "just smile and say you love it."

A knock on the window made him nearly hit his head on the roof of the car. Kayla stood there grinning at him, and he opened the door and stepped out. "Sorry," he said, "I was lost in thought. Do you ever do that?"

She laughed. "All the time." She turned and started walking toward the house. "Come on in." He followed her inside the house, noticing how Sam hurried up the stairs to the left. "Would you like a basic tour?" she asked.

"That would be nice." He looked around the foyer in admiration. "Beautiful home you have."

"Thanks," Kayla replied. "This is the foyer," she said with a raised arm. Then she giggled and her cheeks turned a lovely shade of pink. She walked over to a set of double doors. "This is the office."

He peeked inside. The office was at least twice the size of his bedroom in his trailer where he lived now, which was bigger than the one he had at his last apartment in Denver.

They moved past the office, made a sharp right turn and headed down a short hallway to the living room. His eyes widened at a space that was as large as his entire trailer and was decorated with white leather furniture, a bearskin rug, and a light oak coffee table with matching end tables. A massive fireplace adorned one wall and large plate-glass windows allowed the sun to light up the entire room.

They then went into a huge gourmet kitchen with a long granite-top island, four stools and a breakfast nook with a table for four.

However, what caught his immediate attention were the large windows that looked out across the horizon.

"Wow!" he exclaimed. "You can see the lake and mountains from here!" He cringed when he realized he sounded like an excited child.

However, Kayla did not seem to notice. "You sure can," she said proudly. "As a matter of fact, you can walk straight to the lake from here."

"I didn't notice this lake on the town's website."

"No, you wouldn't. It's private. But if you ever want to use it, just let me know. I can get you in." She laughed and then covered her mouth.

A small snort came from behind him and he turned to see Sam standing in the doorway with a scowl on her face.

"I need to change," Kayla said. "Sam will keep you company for a minute."

"Sounds good."

After Kayla left, James glanced around the kitchen. There was more marble in it than most quarries, and the island alone seemed to rival the length of the one at the diner.

"So, Sam, how are you?" he asked in an attempt to break the ice.

"Fine," she replied in a curt tone.

He smiled. "Thanks for having me over. It's very kind of you."

She shrugged and then pulled out a barstool and looked him over. "You ever wrestle?" she asked.

He laughed and shook his head. "No, just lifted weights," he replied. "I've always been naturally big, I guess."

She nodded, seeming satisfied with the answer. "Those are cool tattoos. I want to get one, but my mom won't let me."

"I see," he said. Then he tilted his head and scrunched his brows. "You're kind of young to get one anyway, don't you think?"

Her laugh expressed how silly she thought his reply was. "Yeah, right. Two girls at my school already have one. But no, not me. I can't even go to Denver with some of my friends. It's like living in a prison around here."

James gave her a quick smile. She was no doubt a typical teenage girl, and he knew at this point there was no sense in arguing with her. Plus, they didn't know each other well enough for her to care what his opinion was.

"So, the service at church today was good, don't you think?"

The scowl she presented him was like many he had seen throughout his life. It was deeply-rooted anger, a look he himself had carried for years.

"I thought it was boring," she said in an off-handed manner. "But whatever. I go to keep mom happy. I don't even believe in that junk."

James knew he had to tread carefully, but then Kayla returned, now wearing a green shirt and fashionable blue jeans. She was absolutely gorgeous.

"Okay, so Sam may have told you that I'm not the greatest cook in the world," Kayla said, "but I do have stuff for sub sandwiches. Is that okay?"

James smiled. "Perfect," he replied. "Here, let me help." He followed her to the fridge and within minutes, all the makings for subs were set out across the counter.

"I love ham," James said as he reached for a fork at the same time Kayla did. His fingers touched hers and for a moment he felt an electrical jolt that somehow brought on what he figured was probably one of the goofiest smiles he had ever had. They both moved their hands back at the same time. "Oh, please, go ahead," he said.

"No, you go first."

"I insist," he said. "Your house, your...ham."

They both burst out laughing, and Sam grumbled something unintelligible and grabbed her plate and headed to the table.

James waited for Kayla to finish before he built his sandwich and then headed over to sit with them.

"Here, take a seat," Kayla said, motioning to the chair at the head of the table.

He reached out his hand to pull out the chair when Sam screamed, "That's my dad's seat! Do not sit there!" The glare she gave him could have turned him into a pillar of salt on the spot.

James snapped his hand back. "I'm sorry," he said in confusion. "I didn't mean…"

"Samantha Jo," Kayla said as she rose from her chair as well, "you apologize right now!"

All James could do was stand there, uncertain if he should stay where he was or leave the room.

"No way," Sam spat. "If you're going to invite some strange guy into our house, at least have some respect for dad's seat." Then she burst into tears and ran past James. He could hear her footsteps stomp up the stairs.

"I'm so sorry," Kayla said, clearly both mortified and angry. "I need to go deal with her."

"No need to apologize," James assured her. Maybe he should just leave, but he worried it would embarrass her more.

Kayla shook her head. "She's getting worse. I've been trying to figure out what's wrong, but…" She sighed and pointed behind James. "The door there leads out back. Go enjoy the patio and views. Just make yourself at home, and if you're still hungry, grab all the food you want."

James nodded as she hurried past him and up the stairs. Maybe he needed to be there, if only to give her someone to talk to.

Lord, help them both be able to communicate. And no matter what, remind them to love each other.

Taking his water and his plate, he headed out back.

***

James took up Kayla on her earlier offer and made a second sandwich and had nearly inhaled it. However, that had been fifteen minutes ago, and as he gazed across the mountain range, he wondered if he should go after all. A large umbrella kept the sun off him and allowed him to relax without sweating up a storm. The pool looked tempting, and he thought how nice it would be to go for a swim, but there was no way he'd go that far in his 'making himself at home'.

The door opened and he turned to see Kayla come out with a glass of water in her hand. "I'm so sorry about all of this," she said with a heavy sigh. "We were supposed to have a nice lunch and welcome you to church, and to the community. Instead, you got a ticket to a Jerry Springer Show." She pulled out the chair across from him at the patio table and sat down.

"It's okay," he replied, somehow glad he had stayed. Maybe he was supposed to be there to lend an ear. "I can't imagine the effect of losing her father has had on her. Plus, if that's her dad's seat, then by all means, I won't sit in it."

Kayla looked out across the lake. "It happened two days after her tenth birthday," she said before wiping at her eyes. "Brandon was supposed to come home the following week. The two had made plans to go fishing, but then…" Her voice trailed off and she let out a heavy sigh. "A roadside bomb." She turned and looked at him. "You know in the movies when they show up at the door and tell the family the bad news?" James nodded. "I opened the door and saw the two men in uniform and immediately knew. Sam was in school and I had to get Susan to pick her up." It was quiet for a moment and then Kayla began to sob.

James reached out for an unused napkin and handed it to her.

"Thanks," she said as she took the napkin and dabbed at her eyes and nose.

"I'm sorry for your loss," he said. "I know how it feels to lose someone." He suppressed the memories of his own grief; this was her time to grieve and he needed to allow her to take the reins of the conversation.

She looked at him, her eyes still glittering with tears. "I'm so sorry for your loss, too."

It went quiet for a moment and James was glad she did not ask him more about it.

She turned her gaze to the table. "So, I go up to talk to Sam just now, and she accuses me of disgracing her father by having you here. And it's not just that, it's everything. The rebellion, her anger.

35

She's not the sweet girl she was even a year ago. It's grown worse, and I don't know what to do."

James took a drink of his water to allow him time to pray for wisdom before he spoke. "You know, I was angry once," he said, feeling the words simply fly into his brain and onto his tongue. "Like, all the time angry, not once as in 'for a minute'." This made Kayla smile, for which James was glad. "The root of it was a deep rage. Rage and fear, both of those things are tied together, and I would guess Sam is experiencing both right now."

Kayla sighed. "I know she's angry about her father dying. Do you think that could be all of it?"

"It might be," James replied. "It might be something connected with it, certainly. Just keep loving her, because love will break through any wall. Trust me, I know firsthand."

Kayla smiled and stuffed the used napkin into her pants pocket. "Thank you," she said. "You're right." Then she reddened again. "By the way, Susan said something came up, so she won't be gracing us with her presence, as I'm sure you've already figured out."

James laughed. "That's great. I thought she wasn't going to let go of my arm earlier."

"Yeah, that's Susan." She leaned back in her chair. "But I want to know more about you. Where are you from originally?" James went to reply, but Kayla stood up. "Sorry. Hold that thought. I need to grab my sandwich. Would you like another?"

"No, thanks," he said with a laugh. "I've already had two."

"Right. Be right back." She hurried off and then a few minutes later returned and retook her seat. "Okay. Life story. Go."

He laughed, almost spitting out the water he was drinking. "Well, I was born just outside of Dallas," he explained. "Dad left mom when I was eight. I quit school when I was thirteen to work to help support her. By sixteen I was getting involved with the wrong crowds, and as I got older, my decisions didn't get any better." He shook his head. Kayla was listening intently, her eyes wide. "I ended up moving to Denver and making some friends who I rode with."

"A motorcycle club?" she asked.

"Sort of," he replied. "Just a loose group of friends. I promise I'm safe." He said the last with a raise of his hand as if stating an oath.

"I know," she said matter-of-factly. "Somehow I just know. Please, go on; this is fascinating."

"Thanks," he said with a small laugh. "Six years ago, someone shared the gospel of Jesus Christ with me. At first I thought the guy was nuts, but he kept visiting me and, well, I'm happy to say I've been a Christian for six years now."

"Wow," Kayla said with conviction. "What an awesome testimony."

James smiled. He had left out many details on purpose. One reason was he didn't know the woman well enough to get down to the nitty-gritty of his life. Plus, he had learned early on that people, even people professing to be Christians, still doubted his conversion. It was judgmental and it hurt deeply, but it was a lesson learned that he needed to tread carefully with new people.

"Now, tell me about you," he said, leaning back in his chair.

She held up a single finger, finished chewing her food, and then followed up with a drink of water. "Sorry. Anyway, I was involved with a rough group, as well," she replied. James raised an eyebrow. "Well, it was the cheerleading squad, but just because we were pretty didn't mean we were not tough."

This brought forth a burst of laughter from them both.

"Great point," James said. "Keep going."

"To be honest, I grew up here in Hope's Crest. I won Miss Hopes Crest when I was a junior in high school." She gave him a pointed look when he broke out in a huge grin. "Trust me, it's not that big of a deal."

He laughed. "I didn't say a word."

"Good. Don't." Her grin was mischievous for a second and then she continued. "I met Brandon when I was around fourteen and it was love at first sight. We were the best of friends, and so shortly after high school graduation, we got married." She let out a sigh, and James smiled at her encouragingly.

"Anyway, though I grew up in a Christian household, it wasn't until I was sixteen that I truly became a Christian."

"Oh?" James asked, intrigued. "What happened, if I might ask?"

She nodded and then glanced around as if someone might overhear. "I started hanging out with a few bad apples in school, getting into trouble and such. Then it got worse."

James nodded. Her story was much like his own, though he never imagined her for one to get into trouble. However, looks were not everything, and a beautiful woman could have a dark past. As it were, everyone had some sort of skeleton in their closet. Some were just bigger than others.

Her face was so red, she appeared to have sat in the sun for too long. "I ended up cheating on an end-of-year exam," she whispered.

James bit down on his lip, trying to suppress his smile. He was expecting her to say she had been involved in a huge fight or maybe stealing a car, but cheating on a test? Yet, he could see the innocence in her eyes and knew that it was a big deal to her.

"Well, the guilt ate at me. And finally I prayed about it, knowing I had messed up. I confessed to my teacher and, most importantly, to God. I didn't ask Him to get me out of the mess, just to give me the strength to do the right thing. And it was at that moment that I felt His presence."

"That's great," James said. "It's really wonderful." And he really meant it.

She looked down at her clasped hands. "To be honest, I've been praying to meet someone, and…this is crazy. I've only known you for a few days, and I know I'm your boss, but would you like to go on a date?"

James's heart leapt with joy. God's voice could not have been any clearer. "You know, I've been praying for the same thing," he said. "And I would love to."

"Great," she said as she stood up and gathered their now empty plates. "Um…next Saturday, do you want to go to the movies?"

"You bet," he replied.

Sam yelled something he could not make out from upstairs. That was his cue that maybe he needed to go and let them two hash things out.

"Thank you again for having me," he said as he walked toward the front door. Then he lowered his voice and looked up at the staircase meaningfully. "I'll be praying for you both."

"I'm glad you came," Kayla said. "And drive carefully."

James smiled. "I will. And keep away from those cheerleader gangs," he said causing her to laugh. A minute later he was in his truck driving home, thankful that God answered prayers and that the woman he had shared some of his heart with had not judged him.

Chapter Six

At five on Tuesday morning, James pulled up in front of A Taste of Heaven Diner and parked his motorcycle in one of the many empty spaces. Today would be his first day and excitement ran through him as he thought about the good fortune he had received since first arriving in Hopes Crest a week earlier. He had a home, a job, and even a date with a beautiful woman who also knew God. Life had its ups and downs, and James was more than pleased that things were now on the up.

As he walked up to the front door, Susan came over and opened the door for him. "Good morning," she said as she stepped aside to let him in.

"Morning," he replied.

Betty, who stood behind the counter rolling silverware, gave him a quick wave.

"Carl's in the kitchen," Susan said as she walked over to the coffee maker and poured a pot of water into it. "Good luck today."

James thanked her and headed to the back. Carl was busy prepping for breakfast, and James grabbed an apron he saw hanging on a hook just behind the door.

"Hey, new guy," Carl said with a laugh as he extended his hand.

James took it and gave it a firm shake. "So, what's first on the list?"

"Coffee," Carl replied, patting James on the back. "Want a cup?"

"I'd love one," James said. He followed Carl back out front where they each poured a cup of coffee and sat down on one of the stools.

"So, I came in earlier than normal today to help set up, so I might take off an hour earlier than usual. But you should only need about half an hour for the grills to heat up.

Deborah usually has a lot of the prep work ready to go, and you'll have a bit, like chopping onions and stuff, but mornings aren't usually too bad." He shot James a quick glance. "Sorry, you're probably familiar with prep already."

James nodded. The process was simple and having worked at a diner similar to this one before, it should have been no different.

"Good," Carl replied. "The first rush is always from six to about eight. Then there's a small rush at ten followed by the eleven-thirty to one-thirty run for lunch. By two, the place is pretty dead until dinner, but Deborah will be here for that."

"Are there any popular items I need to make sure are constantly going?"

"Smart man," Carl said with what sounded like a bit of admiration. "Bacon and pancakes. Keep an eye on them and we'll be fine. I'm sure you're going to do good. Kayla said as much."

"Oh?" James took a sip of his coffee to hide the pride he felt that she was pleased with his abilities even before he started his job.

Susan walked by and added, "Honey, she thinks you're great." She had not even looked at him when she said it, and for that, he was glad because he was sure his face was all shades of red—it was heated enough.

"Susan's a good woman and Kayla's best friend," Carl explained. Of course, he would not know that James had already met both of them already. "She's a riot, though. You'll just have to get used to her nosy ways." Carl lowered his voice. "Betty's the same. Women around here thrive on secrets and gossip."

"Carl, you better watch your mouth or I'll let Mindy know what you just said," Betty called out and both men laughed.

"See what I mean?"

"I sure do," James replied. "So, in other words, smile, let the women run the show, and keep busy making food and I'll be all right?"

"Told you he was smart," Susan said as she returned from the back room.

James and Carl made small talk for the next ten minutes, Carl speaking about his pregnant wife and the baby that was soon to be coming into their lives. James smiled at the man, understanding all too well the happiness he was going through.

"Well, chief, as soon as the girls stop yapping, we can start cooking for the customers," Carl said, giving him a wink as Susan headed to the door to unlock it.

"I'll show you yapping, Carl," Susan said, raising her fist and then opening the door. There were already five men waiting, and James followed Carl back into the kitchen. Grills, ovens, prep trays—it was all so familiar, and besides the great hospitality, James was feeling right at home.

A minute later, Susan leaned in through the gap separating the counter area from the kitchen. "Okay, muscles," she said in a serious voice, "I got two plates with double stack, double sunny side, hash browns, 4 bacon."

She slid the order receipt over and James laughed as he hung it up on the clip in front of him.

"You got it, boss," Carl said as he leaned against a back counter. "I'll watch."

James nodded. He loved a challenge and he grabbed the four strips of bacon and threw them on the grill. Next, he went to the hash brown mix and measured out two portions simply by eye and added them to the grill. For the next two minutes, his hands were a blur as more orders came in. Not waiting for Carl, he continued cooking as the first order was ready.

"Order up," he called out and Susan thanked him as she grabbed the plates.

"Hey, James, is my omelet ready yet?" Betty asked as she tapped her pen against the surface of the metal shelf.

"Here you go, ma'am," he said as he gave her a wink.

"Ma'am? I'm twenty-two...sir," she said as he laughed. The job was fun, the people, like Kayla had said, were family.

As James continued to cook under Carl's appreciative smile, his mind went to Kayla. She would be here soon and he looked forward to seeing her. But he reminded himself that she was his boss and he must keep the work atmosphere strictly professional. Time flew by, and true to Carl's words, another rush came at ten. Pancakes were replaced by burgers and hash brown for fries. But nearing eleven, it slowed down to a crawl.

"I have to say, I'm impressed," Carl said with a shake to his head. "I've never seen someone do such a great job. I kind of feel guilty for not helping." Carl had taken off to the back room over an hour ago to eat and watch TV. Though it didn't bother James at all, he couldn't help but laugh at the look of guilt the man wore on his face.

"You're fine. I handled it well I think."

"Sure did," Carl said as he moved over to the grill area. "Anyway, take an hour lunch; I feel bad."

James smiled and then made himself a sandwich, filled a plastic cup with Sprite and headed out front. The weather was far too nice to be spending the hour inside, so he sat down at a bench that had been placed between the diner and the bookstore next door. As he ate, he studied the downtown area, which reminded him of Hill Valley, the town in *Back to the Future*, though there was no clock tower in the park that sat in the center of the square, the street boxing it in as it wrapped around it.

Hopes Crest was a testament to a time in America's past when life was simpler and more wholesome, and living out here was like taking a step back in time. The people were friendly, the town small and inviting, and he loved it. Even the shops were from another bygone era: Retrocade Arcade, Penny's Coffee Shop, and even an old-fashioned video store called Galaxy Video. If he had not seen it for himself, James would not have believed a video store still existed anywhere; yet, there it was, right across the street from the gun shop. Hopes Crest was the quintessential American small town with a wonderful variety of people from all walks of life who, so far as he had seen, got along well and took even the smallest of moments to at least greet each other and smile.

As he finished his turkey sandwich, Kayla pulled up into one of the empty spaces in front of the diner. She got out and her eyes were red and puffy, as if she had been crying. He set his cup behind the leg of the bench and stood up as she walked up.

"Hey, what's going on?" he asked. He barely knew her, but he hated to see people upset.

"It's Samantha," she replied. She glanced up at him and asked, "Can I vent?"

He nodded and then looked around. "Here or somewhere else?"

"Let's go to the park," she replied.

He walked beside her as they crossed the street to the park that made up the center of the square. It was large enough to grow a few trees, a lot of grass, and even a small children's park with a set of swings, a jungle gym, and a slide. It was empty at the moment, but most of the children were in school at this time of day.

They walked over to a bench underneath a large elm tree, which matched the name of the street, and took a seat.

"So, how can I help?" James asked.

Kayla rubbed her eyes with her palms. "Sam and I fought all morning," she explained. "Apparently my daughter's decided she wants to smoke cigarettes. I found a half of a pack in her purse."

James shook his head. "Wow. Well, I never would've thought she would do something like that. She doesn't come across as that kind of kid."

"I know, right?" Kayla said. "She's sweet as pie one minute and then angry the next, and it's killing me." She began to sob and James leaned over and pulled her into him, just allowing her to cry. After a few minutes, she sniffed and sat back up. "I love my daughter, but I don't know what to do or what to say because whatever I'm saying is not working."

James patted her arm, but he had no clue what to say.

She looked up at him. "You must think I'm crazy," she said with a half-smile. "Both times we are able to have a conversation, I'm fighting with my daughter and I'm a blubbering mess. I'm so sorry. I'm honestly not usually this bad."

"Hey, there's no need to apologize. We're friends now, right?" She nodded and it warmed his heart. At some point and for some reason, God had given him a friend, and it was an idea he loved. "When's the last time you two did something together?"

She bit at her lip. "I don't know. I've been so wrapped up in work, and then there's women's Bible study. I guess it's been a few months at least."

"Then take her out. Not as a reward or anything, but just a girls' night out. Do something fun, let loose, and let her know how much you love her. Drive that point in, that you care about her. I think she'll come around eventually."

Kayla seemed to consider his words. "Do you think so?"

James nodded. "Absolutely. I mean...you're cool for a mom. Former beauty pageant queen, cheerleader and, come on, you walked on the dark side by cheating on that test."

She burst out laughing and gave him a light slap on the arm. "Thank you, James," she said, now much calmer than she had been earlier. "I...well, thank you is all I can say. I'll talk to her later and then take her out Saturday."

"Good." James was glad he could help.

"So, how's your first day so far?" she asked, now back to her controlled self. "Are you liking it?"

"I love it," he replied. "I've learned a lot so far. Carl's great, Susan won't stop calling me 'Muscles' and patting my arm, and Betty hates to be called ma'am."

"Oh, my," Kayla replied. "I'm going to have to talk to Susan about keeping her hands to herself." This brought on another bout of laughter.

"It's really not that big of a deal," James assured her as he stood up and she followed suit.

"I know, but still, she's too crazy sometimes." She stood looking awkward for a moment and then added, "Thanks again for listening." Then she gave him a huge hug. In that hug James felt comforted, supported, and even loved. He only hoped that Kayla felt the same.

Chapter Seven

Kayla gave herself a once-over as she looked at her reflection in the bathroom mirror. She had applied a light touch of makeup and her simple purple t-shirt and dark jeans gave her a comfortable but fashionable look. It had been ages since she had been on a date. As a matter of fact, she had not been on one since she and Brandon went out all those years ago, and before that there had been two lunch dates in the school cafeteria with a boy named Doug.

"You can do this," she told her reflection and a wave of emotions ran through her.

Bowing her head, she prayed for a moment and then let out a long breath. She was excited to see James outside of work and enjoy a movie. The plan was to meet up at the theater and then walk over to Penny's Coffee Shop across the street so she could learn more about him. The thought of James riding with a bunch of bikers at some point both scared and excited her at the same time. It was like something out of a movie, and though she was at first taken aback and wondered if inviting him over had been a mistake, she had felt better as he spoke about his eventual conversion. Everyone deserved the benefit of the doubt.

She grabbed her purse from the foot of her bed, stopped outside of Sam's bedroom door and tapped it with her knuckles.

"Just a minute," Sam called out from the other side.

Kayla waited patiently and when the door still hadn't been opened after a full minute, she tapped again.

"Open."

When Kayla opened the door, Sam sat on her bed and the TV was on. "What were you doing?" she asked her daughter suspiciously.

"Just changing into my pajamas," Sam replied with a smile.

Kayla studied her for a few moments, but when she did not see anything to be suspicious of, she returned the smile and walked over to the bed.

"It's early to be in bed," Kayla said. "Are you feeling okay?" She brushed back the dark hair from her daughter's face.

"Yeah," Sam replied. "It's just one of those nights when I want to watch TV and hang out in my pajamas."

Kayla smiled and leaned over to kiss the top of Sam's head. "Okay, I'm getting ready to leave. There's money on the counter for a pizza and a five-dollar tip. No one's allowed over, and if someone knocks on the door…"

Sam laughed. "Mom, I'm not five; I'm almost fifteen."

Kayla nodded, a twinge of sadness hitting her heart. Soon Sam would be sixteen, then a senior graduating from high school and then off to college. The years were flying by and she wished her little girl who used to play in the kitchen was back instead of the moody teenager she was now. But God never gave anyone anything they could not handle, and hopefully Sam would outgrow whatever this was, just as she had outgrown the terrible twos when she was little.

"You're right," Kayla said. "I love you. I should be back no later than midnight."

"Love you, too," Sam replied.

Kayla waved as she walked out the door but then turned back and smiled at her daughter, who smiled and waved back. Dear Lord, but how she loved her!

She sighed as she walked downstairs. The sun was still in the sky as she opened the truck door and slid in behind the steering wheel.

"A date," she whispered as she sat in the silence. Taking a deep breath, she started up the truck and then let out a laugh. Sure, nervousness was close to overwhelming her, but she was also very excited.

***

She found a parking space across the street from the diner and in front of the thrift store located next to Penny's Coffee Shop. She got out of the truck and walked down the sidewalk toward the end of the square where The Five Star Theater was located. Built in the 1950s, it still had the large old-fashioned marquee, but the rest of the theater had not been remodeled since the 1980s.

 Regardless, Kayla still loved it and felt the decor was more classic than outdated. There already was a line, but it was probably more due to the fact that there was only one ticket window and everyone had to line up outside to buy their tickets.

When her eyes fell on James standing with his hands in his pockets and pacing nervously in front of a large poster for an upcoming movie, Kayla had to suppress a laugh. He wore a pair of dress slacks and a long-sleeved button-up shirt which was much more formal than she herself had chosen.

He looked her up and down and his cheeks reddened. "I thought…you know…a date," he stammered and then began to laugh.

She joined in. "I thought…well, you know…casual," she said and then wiped away the tears of laughter from her eyes.

"Well, since you're going casual…"

Her eyes went wide as he reached up and began unbuttoning his shirt. Surely, he was not going to undress right there in front of the theater? Much to her relief, he wore a black t-shirt underneath. He walked over to his motorcycle and placed his shirt in one of the side compartments.

"Much better," he sighed. "I have to be honest. I've never been the type to wear dress clothes."

"I gathered as much," Kayla teased.

He raised an eyebrow. "Is that so?"

"Of course. I mean, your tattoos and motorcycle don't scream Wall Street type to me." A look of hurt crossed his eyes and Kayla felt overwhelmed with guilt. "But it doesn't matter.

Those types are too stuffy anyway." She was relieved when his eyes lit up at her comment.

"Okay, well, shall we?" he asked.

She nodded and they walked up to the ticket window. A few people she knew from church or the diner walked past and she gave a passing "hello". Usually she would stop and talk, but not tonight. No, tonight was her night.

"I'm on a date," she whispered and then let out a giggle.

"What was that?" James asked.

"Oh, nothing," she replied. She could not stop smiling as they waited in line to buy their tickets. The weather was cool but nice and they were both laughing. The night was only going to get better.

"I love your shirt," James said. "Purple's my favorite color."

"Thanks," she said with a giggle. She was finding it difficult to look at him; her nerves were all over the place.

"*Godzilla Versus Bikers* or *Space Babes from Planet X*? They don't sound like new releases to me," James said as they stepped forward in line.

Kayla groaned. "I forgot to tell you," she said, cringing, "once a month the theater shows B-movies from the eighties." She left out the fact that she secretly liked them, although, for a first date, she was now unsure as to whether or not it was the best choice.

He frowned. "You mean to tell me you like these cheap movies?" he asked.

"Well, yeah. I mean…" She wanted to run and hide.

"That's beyond cool!" he said, the frown now replaced by a huge grin. "*Godzilla Versus Bikers* is one of my favorites."

They both laughed and Kayla was ecstatic. Not only were they both believers, they also shared a love for the same type of movies. The night had just started and already she was glad she had taken this new step in life.

***

Kayla watched the screen as the leader of the bikers paced back and forth, a crowbar in his hand.

"Men, there's one thing that stands in the way of our future," he said, and the group of men he was addressing let out a roar as they raised their weapons in the air. "Today may be our last day, but we will go down fighting!" This was followed by another round of approving shouts, and then the motorcycles rumbled to life. The next shot showed the bikers racing down a deserted dystopian-type of street littered with burned-out cars and rubble from nearby crumbled buildings.

Kayla leaned in towards James and giggled. "Is that how motorcycles groups work?" she whispered in his ear.

"No, not even close," he replied.

Kayla smiled as she returned her attention to the movie. The next thing she knew, everyone in the audience laughed as the Claymation Godzilla appeared and the bikers began to attack it with heavy chains and metal poles. She glanced over at James's hand and felt compelled to take it in hers. Was it appropriate? She did not want to send the wrong signals, but at the same time, she felt James would not be one to read more into it.

Butterflies fluttered in her stomach, and then she let out a scream as one of the bikers flew off his motorcycle. A few people around her laughed, and she cringed with embarrassment.

James leaned in and whispered near her, "It's okay. I screamed the first time I saw it, as well."

This time when she returned her attention to the movie, she reached her hand out and placed it on his. Then his large hand gently closed over hers and gave it a soft squeeze. Though some might not think it appropriate to pray while Godzilla was eating a bunch of bikers, she did just that, thankful for the man He had put in her life.

***

Penny's Coffee Shop was busy when Kayla and James arrived after the movie. Unlike the theater, the shop was much more modern with exposed brick walls and contemporary artwork. The music was a bit more new-agy than she preferred, but it was not bad as a background for conversation.

At the moment, Kayla was concentrating on James as he acted out one of the scenes from the movie that had ended just over half an hour ago.

"'Sorry, little lady'," he said in a deep voice to mimic the character, "'but there comes a time in a man's life when he has to face Godzilla. And that time is now!'"

"Bravo!" Kayla clapped excitedly as he took a bow and then laughed as a few others around them applauded, as well.

He retook his seat and laughed. "I still can't believe we like the same movies. I thought…"

She narrowed her eyes at him. "Okay, mister. You thought what?"

"Well, I mean, you're a former beauty queen, and I just didn't think…well…you know…"

"I get it," she replied. "I don't fit the stereotype. You expected this." She stood up and put her hand in the air. "So, like, are you going to the mall or what?" she said in her best Valley Girl impression as she twirled her hair in her fingers and tilted her head to the side.

James burst out laughing and the couple behind them laughed, too. "That was great," he said as she sat back down.

"Thank you. I took drama for two years."

They continued to talk and then Kayla looked at her phone. "Oh, wow, it's already past eleven. I really need to go; it's getting late. Well, a daughter-at-home-alone late, that is."

"I understand," James said.

They headed outside to where Kayla had parked the truck earlier. "You know," Kayla said, "I was really nervous about tonight. It wasn't an easy decision, but I'm glad I did it."

James smiled. "I know it was hard, and…well…um…do you think…if it's not too pushy to ask," he stammered, and Kayla loved how sweet he was.

"I'd love to," she replied, feeling the necessity of easing his nervousness. "What do you have in mind?"

"What about a motorcycle ride?"

She smiled as she opened the truck door. "Yeah, that sounds like fun." She closed the door, started the truck and rolled down the window. "See you at work?"

"You bet," he said.

Kayla was amused, and touched, that he waited patiently for her to leave before he headed toward his motorcycle. He was a true gentleman.

She gave him a wave and headed back home.

Chapter Eight

Kayla finished brushing out her hair and then headed back into the bedroom. She glanced around, wondering where she had put her purse. Remembering that she had set it on the kitchen table the night before, she left her room and walked down to Sam's.

"Hey, sleepyhead," she said after giving the door a few knocks, "Are you ready for today?" She had taken James's advice and set up a mother-daughter day so she and Sam could spend the day together. Just the thought of their time together brought on a feeling of guilt at how little time they had spent together over the past year.

"Mom, I'm down here," Sam shouted from downstairs.

Surprised, Kayla went down the stairs and into the kitchen, nearly falling over in shock. Sam was pouring out a cup of coffee and was already dressed.

"Wow, you're up early," Kayla said as she took the cup from her daughter. "Thanks."

"I thought I'd better make the most of the day," Sam replied as she poured a second cup, which surprised Kayla even more.

"Oh?" Kayla replied. "And why's that?"

Sam let out a theatrical sigh and then turned to face Kayla. "Well, it seems you have someone new in your life now. I'm sure that, since the two of you will be spending a lot of time together, I'll need to take every opportunity I can to see you." She took a sip of the coffee and grimaced.

"Not a coffee fan, huh?"

Sam shrugged. "It's all right."

"Look, honey, I'm not going to spend every minute with James, so you don't need to worry about you and me. We're just casually dating right now, nothing major."

"I heard you on the phone last night with Susan," Sam said. "You're already going out with him again, this time on his motorcycle." Her expression was less than approving. "Real classy, mom." She grabbed her mug and took a seat at the island.

"What's that supposed to mean?" Kayla demanded.

"Let's see," Sam said as if she was thinking deeply about something. "You have known this guy for a week and you're going to ride around on his motorcycle? It looks pretty trashy if you ask me."

Kayla stared at her daughter. "It's not trashy," she said as she tried to keep her temper under control. "And you need to watch your attitude, young lady. Am I not allowed to go on a date?"

"Whatever," Sam snapped. "Do what you want. You don't care what I say." She brushed her hand over her eyes, and Kayla thought her heart would break.

"I do care," Kayla assured her. "But me going on a date with James is not the end of the world. I don't understand why you're so upset."

The glare Sam gave her made Kayla take a step back. "Because you took off your wedding ring!" she shouted. "You've forgotten all about dad. Well, I haven't and I never will!" By the time she finished, tears were streaming down her face, and Kayla quickly pulled her into her arms.

"Honey, I have not forgotten about your father. It's hard on me too, you know? But I need to move on. I've been praying for God to put someone in my life, and then James shows up…"

Sam pushed her away and scowled at Kayla, the tears still running freely down her face. "Don't say that!"

Kayla's eyes went wide. "What?" She had no idea what was going on but seeing her daughter in this state was upsetting her more than ever.

"God did not put this guy in your life," her daughter shouted. "He filled out an application and that's it. Don't use God as an excuse for you to go out with a tattooed freak!"

"I will not have you yelling at me!" Kayla yelled back. She tried to keep her own tears in check but was failing miserably; she never could control her tears when she was angry.

"Whatever," Sam said as she held up her hand. "Let's just go." Then she headed toward the front door.

"Samantha Jo, I am not done talking," Kayla shouted after her daughter. "Get back here." But her words went unheeded and a moment later, Kayla heard the front door slam.

She stood staring at the empty doorway, unsure as to what she should do. In all honesty, she should have canceled today's outing and grounded Sam for her behavior; yet, she found it hard to deny the girl her feelings. Maybe Sam really did feel like she was being pushed into the background, and if that was true, then her anger was, perhaps not justified, but at least understandable.

Regardless, Kayla needed this time today with Sam as much as Sam needed the time with Kayla, so rather than call off their plans, Kayla sighed. Why some prayers went unanswered while others were not was beyond Kayla, and she shot a glance up at the cross hanging above the sink. Once again she prayed for patience, then turned off the coffee maker and headed outside hoping the day would get better somehow.

***

Nearly sixty old-school arcade machines lined the walls of Retrocade Arcade with all sorts of games from *Pac-Man* to *Dig Dug*. It also had a couple of claw machines where one could test his or her luck and hope to win a prize, as well as a Skee-Ball setup.

"A little to the left," Kayla told Sam as she moved the joystick that controlled the claw that hovered over a stuffed panda. They had been at the arcade for over an hour and they both had tried the machine for the last ten minutes with no luck.

"I think that's it, mom," Sam said. She glanced over at Kayla. "Should I release it?"

Kayla nodded, relieved that Sam's anger had dissipated once they arrived at the arcade. The claw slowly dropped down over the panda and rose, the bear dangling by the minuscule belt around its waist before it dropped down into the chute.

"We did it!" Sam shouted as she leaned down to remove the stuffed animal from the slot at the bottom of the machine. She jumped up and down with excitement and then hugged Kayla tightly.

"Yes, we did," Kayla replied with a wide smile. "It only took twenty bucks, but in the end, we won." They both laughed and Kayla brushed back some of Sam's dark hair behind her ear. "So, do you want to go across the street and eat? Then we can plan what to do next."

"I'd like that," Sam replied.

Kayla gave her daughter another tight hug, so pleased to see how happy she was, and then the two walked out and crossed the Town Square. The park was busy with several families having picnics or playing football. A badminton net had been set up in one area and several people stood by and watched a pair batting a white birdie back and forth to each other. The shouts and laughter of children playing on the playground equipment made Kayla smile. She missed the days when she could bring Sam to the park and watch her run around as a happy child. Though things were rocky now, however, she knew that Sam would once again be her happy daughter. She trusted God to answer prayers, and that had been a huge one.

The diner was pretty quiet with only a few customers eating or drinking coffee. Saturdays were typically slow after lunch, so Kayla was not surprised. She and Sam slid into a booth by one of the front windows with her back to the door and Betty walked over to them.

"Hello, ladies," she said in a formal voice. "Welcome to A Taste of Heaven. Is this your first time here." By the time she finished her introduction, she was laughing, probably because Kayla and Sam were also laughing.

"Good one," Kayla said. "How are you?"

"I'm good. Slow, as usual. So, what are you two having?"

Kayla looked over and gave Sam a nod.

"A cheeseburger with bacon, cheese fries and a Coke," Sam said.

Betty turned to Kayla, who held up two fingers. "Make it two."

"Got it," Betty said with a smile. "Give me about ten minutes." Then she snickered. "As if you wouldn't know that."

Kayla laughed as Betty walked away. She caught a glimpse of James through the opening between the service area and the kitchen. A part of her wanted to go say a quick hello to see how he was doing. Not that it had been that long since she had last seen him—fourteen hours to be exact. But still, just to see his smile for a moment would be nice.

"Mom," Sam grumbled, breaking Kayla from her thoughts.

"What?"

"Go and hang out with him. I can go over to Emma's or Kate's."

Kayla shook her head and reached across the table to take her daughter's hand. "No way," Kayla assured her. "You're mine all day." This brought a smile to Sam's face. "So, what should we do after this?"

Sam shrugged. "I don't know. I wanted to go by the thrift store, but I was wondering something else."

"Sure, what is it?"

Sam's eyes lit up. "Let's do something real fun."

"Okay, tell me." This is what Kayla needed, she and her daughter doing things together.

"Let's go home and pack a change of clothes. Then we can head to Denver and go to the mall. Maybe we can even grab a hotel room, order room service and stay up late together."

"Honey," Kayla said quietly, "that's a great idea, but we have church tomorrow."

Sam's smile disappeared. "Oh, yeah. How could I forget." She rolled her eyes. "We wouldn't want to miss that." She slumped down in the booth seat and crossed her arms.

"Hey, why don't you like going all of a sudden?"

"It's not 'all of a sudden'," Sam said. "I've been this way for a while but you've been too busy to notice." Her tone was accusatory, and Kayla did not like it one bit.

"Look, I like Denver, I really do. What if…"

Sam shook her head. "No, it's cool. I can't go with the girls from school and I can't even go with my mom. Pathetic."

"Maybe we can go next Friday after school."

"Nope," Sam grunted. "You have that date with the motorcycle guy." She scowled. "Just forget it, okay?"

"Honey, you have to work with me on this."

"Let's just forget it, please."

Betty came with their food and set it before them on the table. Kayla thanked her, but she did not feel very hungry.

Sam, on the other hand, picked up her hamburger and started eating it with gusto, although she said nothing. Kayla was happy for the peace, even if it was only temporary. Plus, maybe she was not as upset as Kayla had thought. This made Kayla feel a bit better, and she, too, picked up her burger and began to eat.

One thing Kayla knew for certain was that she needed to do something to get this Sam issue under control. She was doing the best she could do, but it felt like a losing battle that seemed to just keep getting worse. As she contemplated her situation, James walked out of the kitchen with a plate in his hand. Just seeing him and his smile made Kayla warm up and drove away the negative feelings. James saw them, smiled and walked over.

"So, are you done for the day?" Kayla asked, giving him a nod.

"I am," James replied. "Deborah just took over the grill and I'm going to chow down on this burger." He lifted the plate. "It looks so good."

"That's why we got one, too," she said, pointing at their half-eaten burgers.

James laughed. "That's because I cooked it."

"Excuse me," Sam said suddenly as she slid out of the seat. "Nature calls."

Kayla laughed as Sam walked away. Then she turned to James. "I had fun last night," she said. "Thank you again."

"I did, too," he replied. "So, how's your day out going with her?"

Kayla turned to look at where the door that led to the bathrooms was located. "Not so great," she replied with a heavy sigh as she turned back around. "It started out with a lot of arguing and fighting, but I think it will all work out...somehow."

"I'm sure it will," James said, leaning a hand against the back of the booth. "Look, I'll leave you two at it. See you tomorrow at church?"

"Definitely," Kayla said. "And would you like to come over for lunch again? I think Susan may show up this time, so you'll have someone to talk to if I have to deal with Sam."

James laughed. "Sure, sounds good." He walked over to the counter and took a seat.

Kayla let out a sigh and then took a bite of her burger. James was right; the hamburger was good and probably because he made it.

A few minutes later, Kayla was surprised that Sam wasn't back from the bathroom yet, so she went to search for her. She stuck her head through the door and called out Sam's name, but no one answered, so she checked the stalls. They were all empty.

"Oh, Sam," she sighed, dread coming over her. She then went back out to the diner.

Patricia, another waitress who worked at the diner part-time was placing several dirty plates in one of the tubs. "Hey, Kayla," she said as she rinsed a rag out in the soapy water to clean off a table, the strong smell of bleach rising in the air.

"Hi, Patricia," Kayla replied. "You didn't see Sam leave, did you?"

"Yeah," Patricia said, "about five, maybe ten minutes ago. Is everything okay?"

"I hope so," Kayla said and then hurried to the table to grab her purse. She headed outside and glanced around, fear beginning to rise. Did Sam run off? Would she jump into some stranger's car? She pulled out her phone and dialed Sam's number, praying she would get an answer.

***

Thirty minutes later, Kayla was in a state of panic. She had checked all the shops and stores on Elm Street in the Town Square and had called Sam's number at least a dozen times to no avail. She got to the truck and slid behind the wheel, unable to stop the flood of images from entering her mind, images of her being kidnapped or even worse.

"God, please, bring her home safe," Kayla prayed.

Her phone rang, and she dug it out of her purse. The ID said it was Joanne Lawrence, the town Sheriff.

"Jo?" she said after hitting the accept button.

"Hey, Kayla. I have Sam. She's safe." Kayla let out a sigh of relief. "I'm on the highway leading to your place. Drive on out; you'll see my cruiser."

"Thanks, Jo," Kayla replied. "I'll be there in a minute." She hung up the phone, put on her seatbelt and reversed out of the space.

It took everything in her power to not floor it before she was out of town. About two miles later, she spotted Jo's SUV on the side of the road, so she slowed and pulled up behind her. Sam sat on the ground with her arms around her knees.

Jo approached Kayla.

"Is she okay?" Kayla asked.

"She's fine," Jo replied. "But I think you should know, I took these off her." She handed Kayla a pack of cigarettes.

Kayla groaned as she took the pack from the Sheriff and threw them in her purse. "I don't know where she's getting them from, but I'll find out and put a stop to it," she promised.

Sam must have heard because she shot Kayla a glare that should have melted Kayla on the spot.

"Look, I'm going to head out," Jo said. "I have a property dispute I need to deal with. If you have any other problems, give me a call."

"Thanks, Jo." Kayla gave her a hug and was thankful that they had been casual friends since high school. Not to mention that Kayla had helped with Jo's election five years earlier.

"Anytime," Jo said. She got into her cruiser and was gone, leaving Kayla and Sam alone on the side of the road.

Kayla walked over, doing whatever she could do to control her rage. "You ran off?" Kayla asked incredulously. "Do you have any idea how worried I was?" Sam said nothing as she glared off across the empty land on the other side of the road. "Why did you run? And why on earth are you smoking?"

"Why do you care?" Sam spat. Her voice was shaky; she was clearly angry.

"Because I'm your mother," Kayla replied. "And contrary to what you may think, I love you and I don't want to see you hurt."

"You don't mean that." Sam began to cry.

Kayla thought her heart would break. She sat down next to her daughter and put her arm around her. "I do, Sam. But something's wrong with us. We fight all the time, you're angry, and I don't know what to do to make it right."

Sam looked up at her, tears running down her face. "Do you really mean that?"

Kayla stared at her in disbelief. "Of course I do!"

"Then stop seeing James."

It was as if Sam had thrown something at her. "What? Why? What's so wrong with seeing him?"

Sam glared. "Because I'm losing you! Don't you see it?" Sam was sobbing and Kayla pulled her into her.

"I told you, you are not going to lose me." Kayla was not sure how else she could prove to her daughter that she was still the most important person in her life.

"Yes, I am," Sam said as she sat back up. "You have known this guy a week, and you're all lovestruck by him. And don't lie to me, mom. I see the way you two smile at each other. I said it earlier; it's been only a week and you already have had him in the house, going to the movies, and you're going on some motorcycle ride alone together. Can you honestly tell me it's going to slow down?"

Kayla's jaw dropped open. Sam was making a good point, but what was wrong with seeing James?

"You're going to see him every day at work. Then there will be Sunday lunches, Friday night dates. But I'm supposed to believe in between you're going to make time for me? I don't believe you."

Kayla could only stare at her; she loved her daughter more than anything, and to know that she felt this way about Kayla's dating made her stop and think. "I love you, and I don't want to hurt you…"

"Then stop hurting me!" Sam shouted. "I want my mom, not stupid cigarettes or the other crap I'm doing." She looked at Kayla with pleading eyes. "Can't I just have my mom back?"

Kayla pulled her daughter into her arms. Her mind raced as it played the events of the past week in her head. She had gone on a date, invited him to her house again, and was already planning a second date. Perhaps they were moving a bit too quickly. She had been so focused on her own loneliness that she had forgotten her daughter's.

"Okay," Kayla said finally. "I will stop dating for now. We can work on us."

Sam's eyes went wide. "Promise?" she asked.

It pained Kayla immensely to make that promise, but she needed to put her daughter first.

"I promise," she said, and Sam's smile returned, brighter than ever.

Chapter Nine

James stood next to his old truck in the church parking lot and checked his phone again. Kayla had sent him a text asking him to meet her before the service started, and he found it odd that she asked they meet in the parking lot of all places. However, church services would be starting any minute, and he had yet to see her arrive. He hoped everything between her and Sam was better and wondered if she needed some advice. Of course, what advice he could give her he had no clue, but at least he could listen if she needed a ready ear.

Finally, her black truck rolled into the lot, and a minute later both Kayla and Sam got out. Sam headed inside as Kayla came walking up to him, the skirt of her blue dress fluttering around her legs. The sun seemed to brighten her red hair and he reveled in how beautiful she truly was, both inside and out.

"Hey," she said hurriedly, "thanks for meeting me." James was unsure what it could be, but something was off. Her eyes were bloodshot and puffy and her face looked exhausted.

"Of course. Is everything okay?"

She looked down at the ground. "I need to tell you something, and it's not easy."

Fear tried to overtake him, but he pushed it away.

"Right now I'm having a lot of issues with Sam, and I don't think it's fair that you and I continue dating with all that's going on right now. I hope you can understand."

James had known Kayla and Sam were on edge around each other, he had seen it for himself, but he could not help but wonder if he had done something wrong. "Oh, I see." What more could he say?

It was not as if he had come across this issue at any other time in his life, nor did he know anyone who had experienced it. Sure, he had broken up with other women, not many in the past few years, but enough over his lifetime to know it still hurt. What was different about dating Kayla was that it felt as if everything was going so well and now the rug had been pulled right out from under him. It was a strange, and disconcerting, feeling.

"Look, I like you a lot," Kayla continued, "and that's part of the problem. I mean, we've barely known each other for a short time, and then I invited you over to the house, the dates…" She wiped a tear from her eye, and James wished he could just pull her in for a hug but knew it would only make matters worse. "I loved it, but I can't do it anymore. But if things get better soon between Sam and me, and if you're still interested and haven't moved on to someone else, I'd love to go on another date. I just can't right now."

He placed a hand on her shoulder. She was now sobbing, and all he could do was glance around hoping no one thought they were fighting. Not that he cared what other people thought about him—let them gossip—but he was worried about Kayla.

"I understand," he said, which in all honesty he did. It had to be difficult for Sam to have to share her mother after all this time having her to herself. "Your daughter has to come first, and I will be waiting for you. There's no rush, so take your time. I really hope that things work out between you two."

Kayla smiled and then reached into her purse to grab a tissue. "Thanks. I really appreciate it." Then she glanced up at him. "Hey, you're not going to quit on me at the diner, are you?"

He laughed. "I was thinking about it. I mean, I didn't need the job; I just got it to meet you." At first, he worried she had not caught the teasing tone in his voice, but then she smiled broadly at him. The sound of the band starting up made them both turn toward the church doors.

"Well, I better get back inside," she said as she dabbed at her eyes one last time. He was glad she had stopped crying; he was a sucker for a crying woman. "See you on Tuesday?"

"You bet," James said, giving her a quick smile. He watched her walk inside and he leaned against his truck. Right when God seemed to put a woman in his life, she was gone. Well, not completely, he would see her at work, but he had looked so forward to getting to know her on a personal level. It had been years since he had a girlfriend, especially since he had been saved, and he so desperately wanted a companion.

Was this a sign that the door was closed on this particular relationship? And if so, was it permanent? Maybe God had other plans for him, another woman who would come into his life.

"Hey!" he heard someone call from a couple of cars down. Susan was waving him over with a laugh. "Come on! We're already late, and trust me, everyone notices when someone enters after the band has started."

A small thought that Susan might be one that God had placed in his life flashed in his mind, but it was gone as quickly as it came. Susan was a laugh, but James knew in his heart of hearts that she was not for him, not in the romantic sense. No, what he had felt with Kayla was simply not there when he was with Susan.

He smiled at the woman he knew would only be a good friend and followed her into the church. The only way he would know God's plan was to continue to pray, trust in God, and wait for the right door to open.

***

"I can't thank you enough for inviting me over for lunch, preacher," James said, taking a seat at the patio table in Pastor Dave's backyard. He lived in the neighborhood next to James's trailer park, and though the homes were nowhere as big as Kayla's, they were still nice. And Dave even had a pool.

"No need to thank me," he said. "And please call me Dave. Pastor or preacher makes me feel old." He laughed as he turned the hot dogs on the grill.

"Okay, Dave it is," James said with a laugh.

Dave smiled and then turned back to the grill. "I'm sorry that my wife isn't here, but she had to make a trip up to the hospital. Poor Janie Briggs fell off her horse yesterday and had to be admitted."

"I'm very sorry to hear that," James said. He remembered Dave mentioning it during the services asking everyone to add the woman to their prayer lists.

"Well, God's will be done," he said as he placed a platter of food down in the middle of the table. James's eyes went wide; there were both hot dogs and hamburgers on the plate, and potato chips and baked beans already sat in bowls on the table.

Dave chuckled. "I may have overdone it."

James laughed as well. "Let's pray." They lowered their heads and closed their eyes, and Dave thanked God for their food and prayed for those who were in need, including Janie Briggs. "All this in Jesus's precious name, Amen."

"Amen," James repeated.

"All right, dig in."

James grabbed a hot dog and bun and loaded up his plate with food. "This looks great. Thanks again for inviting me."

"No problem at all," Dave said as he grabbed a hamburger and spooned out some baked beans onto his plate. "So, how are you enjoying our little town so far?"

"I like it," James replied. "I have a new place to live, a great job, and…well, everything's going pretty well." He took a bite of the hot dog.

Dave scrunched his brows. "You seemed to hesitate. Is anything wrong?"

James took a drink from his Coke as he pondered whether or not he should tell the man about Kayla. However, Dave was his pastor now, so it made sense to discuss personal issues with him and maybe even get some advice. "As it is, I started seeing this woman. Well, not seeing her exactly, we just went on a date."

"Kayla, right?"

James studied the man. "How did you know?"

Dave laughed. "I was in the back row during the screening of *Godzilla Versus Bikers*." He leaned in conspiratorially. "But don't tell anyone. Cheesy movies are my secret vice." He gave James a wink, which caused both of them to laugh.

"Yeah, it's Kayla. See, I've been praying that God would put a woman in my life, and I thought it was Kayla. We seemed to hit it off from the start. Even during the interview, there was something there. But she and Sam are having some issues, and I think Sam believes I'm taking her mother away from her. So, this morning, Kayla asked that we take a step back so she could repair her relationship with her daughter. It makes perfect sense, but...I don't know, I guess I'm a little bummed out. I really like her."

"Teens," Dave said with a shake to his head, "they are a tough lot. I sent mine off to college two years ago, but those teen years were definitely a challenge."

"I gathered as much," James said.

"So, no kids?"

James took a deep breath, unsure as to how to answer. Dave seemed to pick up on his hesitancy and quickly changed the subject, for which James was relieved. He wasn't sure if he was ready to rehash some of his past.

"Let me give you some advice," Dave said. "If you don't mind, of course."

"Please. I'm feeling pretty confused right now."

"A lot of the time we don't know how God's plan is going to work. We love to speculate, but sometimes when we think it's going one way, all of a sudden it goes another."

This was not new information to James. "Exactly. Many times it keeps me guessing."

"What you need to do is stay focused on the Lord. Whether you are meant to date this woman or not, I don't know. But keep her and Sam in your prayers. Besides that, you can only wait. It may not be what you wanted to hear, but I think it's what you need to hear.

We live in an age when we want everything right now, but our time is not always God's time. However, if we trust in Him, it always works out for the better."

"Good stuff," James said.

"Have some more," Dave said, indicating the food that was still piled on the table.

"Thanks, I think I will." James reached over and grabbed another hot dog. Dave's eyes were on the tattoo on James's forearm and he quickly pulled his hand back.

"How long were you involved?" Dave asked as he nodded at James's arm.

James held his breath. He did not want to lie to the man, but experience taught him that by telling him the truth could be a sure way to be shown the door.

However, before he could give even a flimsy explanation, Dave said, "Tell you what, let me tell you a story." He wiped his fingers on a napkin, pushed his plate aside, and crossed his arms on the table. "It's about a young man and the woman he met at a strip club."

James's jaw dropped open. "You mean...?"

"That's right. I was a bartender and Maria was a waitress. Both of us would get high after work in the parking lot. We ran off and got married, had a daughter, and was on the fastest path to Hell imaginable." For some time Dave shared his life story of how both he and Maria came to know the Lord and how he eventually went to seminary. It was encouraging and made James respect the man even more. "So, I tell you all about that to say that I don't care what you did in your past life. You are a new creation in Jesus. So, if He has forgotten your past and does not judge you, then neither do I."

James let out a deep breath as his mind began to swirl. There was so much to tell and he wasn't sure where to start.

"I guess when I first saw the guys on the bikes and the women on their arms, I was about twenty or so. I was instantly attracted to the idea, and before I knew it, I was a member. But it didn't stop there. Over the years, I worked my way up, so to speak." The memories came as if they had happened yesterday.

"Then I met Vicki, and she was as wild as they come." He continued with his story for the next hour; it had been a very long time since he had been able to share his past with someone else without fear of being judged for it, and when he was finished, he looked up to see Dave smiling.

"So, am I still allowed at church?" James asked, half joking.

"Are you kidding me?" Dave gasped. "That's one of the greatest testimonies I've ever heard." He stood up and James followed suit, his heart happy for the first time in a very long time. "I'll tell you what...let's go inside and get some cake Maria made. I'm not supposed to eat it until she gets back, but this calls for a celebration."

James stared at the man. "Celebration?"

"Your testimony's the answer to your dilemma. It's just more proof that God opens doors when we think they're closed for good."

Smiling, James realized the man was right. He followed Dave into the house. Although he had no idea what God had in store for him, no matter what it was, God was going to be there for him, he had no doubt at all about that fact.

Chapter Ten

Kayla let out a sigh as both her daughter and Emma stood before her. It was a Friday night and Kayla was supposed to be watching a movie with Sam this evening; however, much to Kayla's surprise and irritation, Sam had invited Emma over to stay the night. It was not that Kayla minded Emma being there, but rather it was the fact that Sam had not asked beforehand if Emma could stay. Also, it bothered Kayla that, once again, Sam had canceled plans after all the fuss she had made that she and Kayla had not been spending enough time together.

It had been over two weeks, coming up three, since she had stopped seeing James, hoping it would build bonding time between her and Sam. Instead, every single time they made plans, Sam would come down with a headache or have Emma or one of her other friends over and then insist that they wanted to watch TV in her room.

"I suppose it's fine," Kayla said. "But next time, please ask before you ask her to stay over."

"Thanks, mom," Sam said. "We're going to order a pizza in a bit but we're going for a swim first." Turning to Emma, she smiled. "Come on, let's head upstairs." Emma walked off with Sam following, but Kayla reached out and grabbed her arm before she could leave the room.

Kayla shot Emma a quick glance. "She'll be with you in a moment," she said with a smile. "Go ahead and head upstairs." Emma nodded, and when Kayla was sure Emma was gone, she turned back to Sam.

"What?" Sam asked, her voice a bit more demanding that Kayla wished to hear.

Kayla rubbed her temples as she tried to keep her temper in check. "First off, drop that attitude. Second, you can't bring people over telling them they can stay, then ask me afterward. It defeats the whole purpose of you having to ask."

"Got it," Sam said and went to move past her, but Kayla moved in front of her to block her escape.

"One more thing," she said.

Sam tapped her foot. "Yeah?" Her tone was almost bored, and it took every ounce of power to keep Kayla from slapping her silly.

"What about me and you?" Kayla asked. "I thought we were going to spend more time together. It's been three weeks and we haven't done a single thing."

"There's no rush, is there?"

"No, there isn't a rush, but I want to start seeing James again eventually. That was our agreement, remember?"

Sam's laugh was so contemptuous, Kayla could barely contain herself. "Oh, yeah. Spend time with me then go back to the loser."

"He's not a loser," Kayla seethed. "How dare you."

"Please. He's almost forty and makes hamburgers for a living and lives in a trailer park. Way to aim high, mom."

"Go upstairs with Emma," Kayla commanded. "Tomorrow she goes home and you are back to being grounded. I'm not doing this anymore. Do you understand me?"

Sam nodded. She didn't say a word, though the scowl on her face spoke volumes. "Can I go now?"

"Yes," Kayla said, then watched as Sam hurried past her. Wiping at her eye, Kayla went over to the counter, dug out money from her purse and left it on the counter for the pizza the girls would be ordering later. Then she poured a glass of wine and headed to the office where she closed the door and selected a playlist of her favorite songs on the computer.

As she leaned back in the office chair, she wondered at her own abilities as a mother and a decision maker for her family. Sam had been allowed off her grounding after she promised Kayla she was going to behave, but once again, that had not happened.

Kayla reached over and grabbed the report card that had come in the mail earlier that day. Sam was going to pass this year, but her grades had taken a dive. The more Kayla reached out to her daughter, the more Sam withdrew. From smoking to cutting a class last week, everything was spiraling out of control, and Kayla was at a loss as to what to do about it.

She tossed the report card back on the desk and once again leaned back in the chair. Her mind drifted to James. He would know what to do. He was full of advice and she wanted nothing more than to sit with him and just talk. Of course, she had Susan, but truth be told, Kayla missed James's companionship. It was true she saw him at work every day, and they made small talk that lasted for a minute or so. However, he was a neutral person who could see things from outside—someone who could give her unbiased advice. Yet, beyond the 'hellos' and 'how about this weather?', their short conversations were strained.

Perhaps she had been hasty in her decision to not see him anymore. Maybe God had truly put him in her life and she was now paying the price by ignoring His gift. Closing her eyes, she prayed, asking God not only for wisdom, but for strength, as well.

***

Wednesday night Kayla found herself in Maria's living room surrounded by nearly a dozen women. The monthly ladies' get-together was always a wonderful way to connect with other women and share in what God had in store for them. There was a Bible study and discussion followed by prayer requests and general conversation about what was going on in each other's lives.

Susan was there, and surprisingly, so was Betty. Although Kayla had invited the woman before, this was the first time Betty had taken Kayla up on her offer. Judging by her smile, she was enjoying it, which made Kayla happy. Every woman needed other women in her life for guidance and support.

"Dolores," Maria said, "did you want to share anything." She shot Kayla a wink and Susan groaned quietly beside Kayla. The older woman had returned from her trip to visit her son's family, and Kayla had an idea what was coming.

Dolores stood regally before the group and jutted out her chin. "Frederick and Melissa's home was beautiful, most definitely the largest on the block," she said in the same tone of superiority she often used when discussing her family's achievements.

Susan leaned in toward Kayla. "I bet Dolores had the biggest ego on the block, too," she whispered.

Kayla covered her mouth to stifle a laugh. She knew it was wrong to discuss the woman this way, but she was a respected member of the church and had quite a bit of support within the town. Her family had been there since its founding, or so she had said on more than one occasion.

"Their children were very well-behaved," the woman continued. Then she looked over at Kayla meaningfully for a brief moment and Kayla felt her anger flare. What was she trying to say? The woman finished with, "I had a lovely time and cannot wait to return."

After Dolores took her seat, Maria said, "That's great. Any chance they are coming to visit soon so we can all meet them?"

Dolores sniffed derisively. "I highly doubt it. Frederick is far too busy with his work, and I'm afraid the standards of entertaining guests in this town have become quite poor, to be honest. Which reminds me, have you seen the state of the video store?"

Several more women joined Susan in her groaning as the woman went on for a full ten minutes on ways businesses in the main Town Square could upgrade their storefronts, as well as the inside of their shops. This was the typical Dolores Van Schneider, and everyone let her have her say and then did what they thought should be done anyway.

"Ladies," Maria said as she stood when Dolores had completed her rant, "I want to thank you for coming once again. Betty, I hope to see you again soon."

"Definitely," Betty replied with a wide smile.

"Great. Let's pray." All the women stood and grabbed the hand of the women on either side of them until the circle was complete. A few minutes later, the prayer ended with an echo of 'Amen' and then Maria added, "There's food and drinks in the kitchen, so please help yourself."

Susan walked up to Kayla. "Hey, I'm going to see if Betty wants to come to church Sunday. I'll catch up with you in a minute."

Kayla nodded and then grabbed her purse.

Maria came up to her. "Hey, you," she said as she gave her a hug. "Care to come have a chat with me outside for a minute?"

"Sure," Kayla replied and she followed Maria outside. The sun had just dipped under the horizon and the stars were fighting to break through the last bit of dusk.

"I want you to know that I've been praying for you," Maria said when Kayla closed the door behind her. "How are things?"

"Well, you know teenage girls."

Maria nodded. "I sure do. How about you, though. How are you holding up?"

Kayla bit her lip to keep from crying. She felt like she had done enough crying over the past few weeks to last her a lifetime. "I feel so confused, to be honest. It took me forever to decide to date again, and after so much prayer and then meeting James, it was the answer I was looking for, or so I thought. But then with all the stuff going one with Sam…well, you know how that went down."

"So, what are your thoughts on Sam?"

Kayla sighed heavily. "I don't know. I feel like Sam tricked me to stop seeing James. Was it wrong for me to want to date, even though Sam and I are arguing? Does it make me a bad mom?" The tears started of their own accord, much to Kayla's dismay.

However, Maria did not seem to mind Kayla's tears. "Not at all," she said as she laid a hand on Kayla's arm. "Listen to me. You are a great mom. You support Sam in every way imaginable. I've seen you at the bake sales and the school fundraisers. You go above and beyond for that girl. And yes, I do think she's pulling at your heartstrings to get her way."

Kayla studied Maria's face. "So, should I see James again?"

Maria smiled. "That is between you and God, but I think it's fine."

"But what if Sam acts up again?"

"Look, when Lisa was fifteen, she snuck out of the house. We caught her at Angel Falls with a boy and I thought Dave was going to rip the kid's head off."

"Oh, wow," Kayla gasped. "I had no idea. I thought you and Dave…"

"You thought that Dave being a pastor would mean God gives us extra good kids that never give us trouble?" Maria asked with a bit of sarcasm behind her words.

"Something like that," Kayla replied with a small laugh.

"Honey, teen girls are the worst. We both know that. But the point is, with her ups and downs, we were steadfast in prayer and communication. Keep praying for her, keep talking to her—even when she doesn't respond. In the end, I promise you that the light of Christ is going to shine through and break up that darkness that's surrounding her."

Kayla smiled, wiped at her eyes, and then put her arms around Maria. "Thank you so much," she whispered. "I feel better."

"Anytime. I'm here for you. Love you." Kayla already knew that both Dave and Maria were the biggest blessings in disguise she had ever had, and she loved them dearly.

The back door opened and Susan stuck her head out. "Sorry to interrupt, ladies, but Dolores is driving everyone crazy and trying to drum up support for a Little House on the Prairie marathon for the next meeting."

Maria laughed and turned to Kayla. "I'd better go handle this," she said. "I'll see you in a bit."

Kayla nodded and then a moment later she was left alone out back. Saying a prayer, she let God know how she felt about James and what she wanted to do. Her words turned to Sam and she asked for strength for the months ahead. When she was done, her heart felt joy, the burden weighing down on her all but gone. There was nothing like handing over one's problems at the feet of the Lord.

Looking up at the sky, a wide smile came over her face. Though the night was dark, the stars had won the battle and their light shone brightly as they decorated the sky. Just like Maria said minutes earlier, with patience and prayer the True Light would shine through, much like the darkness between her and Sam.

Chapter Eleven

Lunch had finally slowed, and James plated the last order of the rush—a burger and fries. "Order up," he said as he set the plate on the counter.

"Thanks, sweetie," Susan said as she grabbed the plate.

James laughed. She would call him sweetie, or her favorite—muscles—but rarely his given name. In the beginning, he thought she was coming on to him, but the more time he spent with her, the more he realized that she just enjoyed being silly. They had shared a few lunch breaks together and he found he enjoyed her company, but it would never be more than a friendship, of that he was certain.

"Hey, boss," a voice said from the kitchen door. "You got a minute?" Carl hadn't been in since leaving the diner the day his daughter was born, and that was several weeks ago.

"Sure," James replied as he scraped down the grill. "Let me ask Deborah if she's ready and we can sit down and have a chat." They walked down the short hallway to the break room where Deborah sat watching a soap opera on the TV mounted on a far wall. "Hey, Deborah, do you mind if I cut out a few minutes early?"

She glanced over and smiled. "Hey, Carl." Then she looked at James. "Sure. I hate this stuff anyway." She pointed the remote at the set and turned it off.

"Thanks," James said. "I already stocked everything and the grill has been scraped. The only things left are the things you usually do anyway."

"Sounds good," Deborah replied. "Have a good one." She walked past them and headed to the kitchen. Soon, the sounds of chopping resounded down the hallway and James knew she was already starting on the soup for the evening.

"Come on in and sit down," James said. "Do you want anything? Maybe a drink?"

Carl took a seat at the round cafeteria-style table. "Nah, I'm fine. But thanks."

James sat across from Carl and smiled. "How's life being a dad?"

Carl beamed. "Man, it's great. They are a joy, aren't they?"

James's smile faltered a bit, but he said nothing, although his heart tore just a little inside. He pushed the memories that threatened to return back into the recesses of his mind. "They are," he replied. "So, what's up?"

The room grew quiet, the only sound the rhythmic *chop, chop* of Deborah's knife in the kitchen. "Well, I'm quickly realizing that I can't stay away from work anymore. We thought we'd saved enough for me to take more time off, but the bills are piling up and our savings has dropped down a whole lot faster than planned. I can't believe how expensive having a baby is! Plus, I don't know if you heard, but Mindy had complications during the birth, so the hospital bills ended up being higher than we had budgeted for."

James understood all too well how Carl felt. Although he had a healthy savings account, small incidental purchases and repairs to the trailer had stretched his budget pretty thin. If he had to include the costs of supporting a wife and a baby, he would be in the same boat.

"So, I was wondering…do you think there's a chance I could have your Saturday shift? And maybe a few hours on Friday?" Carl leaned forward. "Look, I don't want to just come in and take back over my job; that wouldn't be fair. But I'm really in a bind here."

How could James deny a family what they needed? "You got it," he replied. He would just have to readjust his own budget and make it work. "If you need more hours, let me know. I can maybe give you another day." It hurt to say as much, but he could make it work somehow.

There was no way he could say no to a man who looked at him with such desperation on his face. Plus, James knew God would provide; He always did.

Carl relaxed exponentially. "Man, you are something else," he said. "I was worried you might say no."

James smiled. "Just bring that little girl of yours by sometime; I would love to see her."

"I will," Carl promised as he shook James's hand. "Thanks again. I'm going to go tell Mindy." As he walked out of the break room, he had a bounce to his step that James realized had been missing when the man had entered.

On his way out to the dining room, James peeked in the kitchen and said goodbye to Deborah, who waved at him with a spatula in her hand.

"See ya," he called out to Susan.

She glanced up from the table she was cleaning and waved at him as he walked out the front door.

It felt good to be outside again. As much as he loved his job, he loved the outdoors that much more. It was why he preferred his motorcycle to the truck. Sure, the truck could get him where he needed to go, and provided cover when it rained or snowed, but he preferred the open air on his bike.

As he glanced around the Town Square, he decided to head over to the arcade and play some Pac-Man.

Granted, he was losing a few hours of work very soon and his budget would be much tighter, but it was an activity that was fun and relaxing. After that, he would grab a pizza to take home. Fishing had sounded appealing, but with all that had been happening with Kayla, he felt uncomfortable with asking about using the private lake by her house.

One thing he did not want was to interfere with Kayla and her daughter. Besides, Lake Hope was close to the trailer park he could fish in, even if it was not as nice as Kayla's private lake.

The thought of Kayla brought a longing to his heart. She was so precious and he thought back to their single date a month ago.

It had seemed like years, but he could still feel the warmth of holding her hand. It was soft and gentle, and it felt so right in his own hand.

"That's a big smile," a voice said as he entered the park. "What're you thinking about?"

James turned and he felt his face heat up when he saw Kayla standing only a few feet away. Her head was tilted ever so slightly and her hand was on her hip. The way the sunlight shone on her, James could have sworn she walked off the canvas of a painting. The green blouse matched her eyes.

"Uh, just stuff," he said and then laughed.

"I see. How are you?"

"Good," he replied. "I take it Carl asked you about taking over my Saturday shift?"

Kayla nodded as she took a step toward him. "He did. I take it you're going to give it to him?"

"I am. He needs the money and with a new kid, I couldn't say no." The way Kayla smiled made him want to join her in it, so he did.

"I guess we're both full of smiles today," she said. "But, unlike you, I'll tell you why I'm smiling."

He gave her a half-smile. "I'd love to hear it," he said, and the two began to walk down the sidewalk together. Kayla waved at a few people she knew, calling them by name. Quite a few tourists were in the park, though the season would not start for at least another week.

"I've been doing a lot praying and thinking," Kayla said, "about me and Sam...and even you."

They took a seat on one of the benches in a far corner of the park under a large tree. It was a quiet spot away from the other people enjoying the warm weather, for which James was glad. Kayla bit at her lip nervously and looked down at her hands.

"I see," James said, trying to keep a feeling of foreboding away. When Kayla did not expand on the topic, he added, "You can tell me anything." Then it hit him. "Am I fired?"

She laughed. "Oh, no," she assured him. "Not even close. I...if it's okay with you, I'd love to go on another date with you.

I really enjoy your company, and I want to spend time with you, but I have to warn you about a few things."

Relief washed over him. He still had his job, and she wanted to date again. The idea excited him, and he was willing to take on whatever complications that came with it. "Sure, what is it?"

"My life is upside down right now," she said. "I'm dealing with a teenager who's driving me crazy and who's going to throw a fit whenever I invite you over. I won't tolerate her bad behavior toward you, but I must warn you, it may come. Also, I tend to talk a lot, and I can get really cranky sometimes, especially when Sam and I are fighting. I may have to cancel dates with you at the last minute in order to keep an eye on her. But if you're willing to put up with all that, I would love to start dating again." She seemed out of breath by the time she finished.

James smiled and took her hand in his. He gazed into her green eyes and saw how beautiful they were, how innocent her face was. In all honesty, what he really wanted to do was kiss her, but it was far too early for that. "I'd like nothing more than to hang out with you. So, yes, I understand what's going on at home, and I get I will be stood up like a nerd on prom night. But to see you again, even once in a while, it's worth it."

"Aww," Kayla said. Then she leaned in to give him a hug. "Thank you. That means so much."

When they stood, he offered her his hand and she took it with a wide smile.

"Speaking of a date, I was going to play some Pac-Man. Would you care to watch me for a bit?"

Kayla gave him an offended look. "Watch? I will have you know that I'm the Pac-Man champ," she said as they walked across the street to Retrocade Arcade.

"Really?" he asked. "I wouldn't have thought that about you."

She raised an eyebrow at him. "There's a lot you don't know about me, Mr. Tough Guy," she said indignantly. "I'm not as sweet as I look."

This brought on a bout of laughter, and James looked down at her, his heart skipping a beat. They were still holding hands, but unlike the nerd on prom night, he was not being stood up, and he was thankful for it.

***

James watched as Pac-Man ran right into another ghost and Kayla let out a groan followed by a laugh. "You know," James teased as he raised a single eyebrow, "for a video game champion, you're sure not having much luck."

She put her hand on her hip and shot him a glare. "Are you criticizing me?"

"No," James said, raising his hand as if to defend himself. "I'm not dumb enough to pick a fight with a cheerleader." They both laughed and then James's stomach rumbled. He closed his eyes in embarrassment, but Kayla laughed.

"Okay, hint taken," she said. "Do you want to grab some lunch?"

"Definitely," he replied. They walked over to the snack bar, and a few minutes later, he sat at one of the four booths, each with bright orange faux leather covering them, and set down a Coke and a plate piled high with nachos. Kayla, apparently not as hungry as he was, ordered just a small basket of fries.

"So, tell me more about you," Kayla said, taking her fry and dipping it in the cheese sauce on his nachos.

"Sure, what do you want to know?"

"Have you been married before?"

He crunched down on a chip and then followed it with a drink in an attempt to collect his thoughts. He did not want to lie to her, but he also was not ready to share with her some of those dark aspects of his past.

Kayla must have picked up on his hesitancy because she said, "I'm sorry. I'm being way too nosy."

"No," he replied with a sigh. "It's fine. If we're going to be dating, then maybe we should know a little bit more about each other.

I was with a woman named Vicki for quite a few years." He decided not to mention that they were together for ten years.

"So, you dated the whole time?"

He smiled. Some people might find her digs for information annoying or meddlesome, but he did not feel that way. He thought it was nice she wanted to know more about him. Plus, she was not coming across as nosy but more as if she was curious, and there was nothing wrong with that. "Yeah," he replied. "It was pretty serious, but we never got married."

He could feel his face heat up. It was funny how he could be embarrassed that he lived with a woman without being married. If it had been even fifty years earlier, people might have been shocked, but in today's world, it was much more accepted. That did not mean he thought anyone should simply move in together just because it was what people did, but his views on relationships had changed enough to realize that, without an open commitment, most relationships could easily fall apart. Granted, not all, but many. No wonder God pushed for marriage so much.

Kayla, however, did not even bat an eyelash. Instead she simply nodded, seeming content with his reply.

"Do you want to know why we broke up?" he asked.

She stopped, a fry in her fingers only inches from her mouth. "Sure, if you want to tell me. But I don't need to know if it makes you uncomfortable."

He leaned in, gave a heavy sigh, and then pursed his lips. "She stole some nachos off my plate," he said and then glanced down. Kayla's hand was holding one of his chips.

Her eyes went wide and she sat frozen as she stared at him.

"You're too easy to fool," he said with a laugh. She popped the chip into her mouth and smiled as he continued. "No, it came down to when I got saved; she wanted nothing to do with it. I gave it time, tried to be patient, to see if she would join me in my walk, but she wouldn't even talk about it. Eventually, we parted ways. Pearls before swine and all that."

He sighed. He had loved Vicki, but it was more than just her lack of, or subject of, conversation. It was years of painful memories, anger, and a host of other problems he did not care to discuss in a snack bar.

Kayla nodded. "Yeah, that makes sense. Sorry it ended that way." She grabbed another chip, this one with a large dollop of nacho cheese on it. "Thanks for the nachos," she said and went to put it in her mouth only to miss.

James laughed. She had not even noticed that she had gotten cheese on her cheek, and he leaned over and wiped it off her face. "There," he said, and her cheeks reddened. He leaned back into the seat, pushed out his stomach and patted it. "Nothing like a healthy plate of nachos. I'm going to have to start packing a lunch or I'm going to be huge."

"Oh, please," Kayla said with a laugh. "There's no way that ripped body's going to get fat." Then she gasped, her eyes wide, and covered her mouth in shock. The redness of her cheeks deepened to such a degree, if James did not know better, he would have worried she was choking on something.

Wanting to save her from further embarrassment, James changed the subject. "So…one more game of Pac-Man before we leave?"

She nodded, though her face was still deeply flushed, but then her phone buzzed and vibrated on the table. She picked it up and looked at the screen. "Darn," she sighed. "I need to go get Sam from school."

He stood up when she did and then walked her outside to her truck. "That was fun," he said, motioning at the arcade behind him. "We should do it again sometime—if you want, that is."

She raised an eyebrow at him. "Are you asking me out?"

He stuck out his chin defiantly. "I am," he replied firmly. "Are you accepting?"

"I am."

They both laughed and he opened the truck door for her. Kayla slid in behind the steering wheel and closed the door. "Before I forget," she said, "school's out on Friday, and though I probably shouldn't because of her behavior, I'm throwing an end-of-the-year party for Sam.

It's tradition. Anyway, do you want to come?"

"Sure," James replied. "That sounds like fun."

She smiled. "Great. Well, maybe I'll send you a text later if I don't see you before then."

"I'll be waiting," he replied.

She waved as she started the truck and then reversed out into the street. James watched her drive away in wonderment. Just when he was thinking the door had closed on a relationship with Kayla, it once again was opened. He pulled out his phone and called Pastor Dave to tell him the good news.

Chapter Twelve

The sun shone brightly Friday just after noon as Susan and James helped Kayla set up for Sam's party. James was moving one of the tables for at least the fourth time and Kayla had her face covered with her hand as Susan snickered.

"Just a half-foot to the left," Susan called out. James nodded and moved the table again.

"Susan," Kayla hissed, "stop it, right now!"

Susan turned to her and grinned. "Sorry," she said as she raised her hand to show her sincerity. "I'll stop." She called over to James. "That's good. Thanks, handsome."

Kayla could not stop a giggle as James walked up to them and she tried to cover it with a cough.

"Okay," James said, obviously missing Susan's comment, "what next?"

Kayla loved this man's willingness to help and the eagerness in his eyes let her know it was genuine.

"Kayla needs her house painted," Susan teased. Kayla gave her a soft elbow to the side, but this only made Susan laugh.

"I think we're good," Kayla said, shooting Susan a glare that she hoped would get the woman to behave herself. Susan had always been the same way and it broke Kayla's heart to know that Susan's husband had walked out on her three years ago. Though it had crushed the woman, she managed to move on and her happy demeanor had returned within a year.

They had been working for over an hour setting up five tables, filling coolers with bottled water and soft drinks, and preparing food for a barbecue. The guests were not to arrive until three, but they were pretty much ready to go. School was due to let out early, but Sam was going to Emma's and then both girls would be here in time to welcome their friends.

Susan shot Kayla a glare. "Hey, we've been working our butts off," she said in mock annoyance. "Are you going to make us some lunch as a way of payment?" A tiny smile played on her lips.

"Sure," Kayla replied, "it's the least I can do." She led them inside, went to the fridge and pulled out three pre-made subs she had picked up earlier that morning from the deli in Hammond's Grocery. After setting them on the counter, she grabbed a bottled water for each of them. "There," she said as she swiped away imaginary sweat from her brow. "That was a lot of work." They all laughed and she took a seat between James and Susan.

"Great sub," James said after his first bite. "You are amazing in the kitchen."

Kayla gave him a small bow. "Thank you," she replied. Then she narrowed her eyes at him. "I do cook, by the way."

"Sure you do, hon," Susan said, giving her a wink. "So, James, you've been here just about a month or so. What do you think of our little town?"

"I love it," James replied as he set his sub down on the open wrapper he was using as a plate. Kayla winced. She could have at least offered him a plate, but he did not seem to mind. "Good people, great weather; though I heard winter's going to be a mess."

Kayla nodded. "You have no idea. The single plow in town does a good enough job, but we will have what?" She turned to Susan. "Two? Three days of being snowed in?"

"You know that's right," Susan replied.

Kayla turned her attention back to James to say something else but went quiet when she saw him staring at her. The man was extremely handsome and his brown eyes were so kind, it just made her heart melt. It was as if time had stopped and only the two of them existed at that moment, the rest of the world suddenly having disappeared.

"Are you two playing the staring game," Susan asked, startling Kayla, who wanted to strangle the woman for popping that bubbled heartbeat of time.

"We were until you interrupted," Kayla snapped at her, but her tone was playful. She knew Susan had not meant to break that connection.

They continued to eat as they made small talk, and when Kayla looked back over at James, he gave her a wink. And for the first time, she considered that this dating thing might just eventually become something much more serious.

***

The next few hours flew by, and soon guests began to arrive. Thankfully, Susan was there to help guide everyone around the house and keep an eye on the teens outside in the pool. It was thirty minutes past three and Sam had yet to show up. Kayla was about ready to call Sam and find out where she was, but then she walked into the house, followed by Emma and a woman Kayla did not know.

"Hey, mom," Sam said. "This is Emma's mom, Molly." The woman appeared to be Kayla's age and extremely pretty. She dressed more like a member of a rock band than a mother, with a dark tank top with a contrasting white skull on it, lots of silver jewelry, dark jeans that appeared to be painted on, and boots. However, it was not the form of dress Kayla noticed but rather the multicolored tattoos that covered both of her arms.

"Nice to meet you," the woman said as she extended her hand out to Kayla.

Sam and Emma did not stick around but instead rushed out to the pool to meet up with their friends.

"Hello," Kayla replied. Then when she realized she was standing there staring at the poor woman, she motioned to James, who came over with a wide smile on his face. He had been so great as she introduced so many people, there would be no way he would remember everyone's names. "This is my…friend James."

"Oh, hello," Molly said in an overly sweet voice as she shook James's hand. The woman's hand instantly went to her hair and she began twirling it between her fingers, and something hit Kayla, catching her off-guard and sending her mind in a million different directions, something she had not felt in a very long time. Jealousy.

"Here, let me show you around," Kayla said, stepping between James and Molly and placing her hand on Molly's shoulder. She was not sure, but she would have sworn she heard James snicker as he followed behind them. After giving Molly a quick tour of the house, she guided her through the back door and out to the pool area. Some of Sam's classmates were already in the pool tossing a beach ball or splashing one another as Susan watched over them from a nearby lounge chair.

She offered Molly a water, and Molly took it from her. "Thanks again for having us over," she said as she twisted off the lid of the bottle. "It's been good for Emma being here. I'm sure you know that her dad and I are recently divorced."

"Emma mentioned," Kayla replied, "and having Emma here is not a problem. She's a sweetheart and we love having her over."

"Oh," Molly said with a glance at James, "so you live here?"

Kayla laughed. "No, he doesn't," she replied. "We, as in Sam and I."

Molly smiled and then turned to James. "Love the tats, by the way," she said, that cloying voice having returned, much to Kayla's annoyance. "Like my sleeves?" She turned slightly to display a tattoo of a deep red rose with leaves and vines around her upper right arm.

James leaned in for a closer look. "Wow, the detail's great," he said in clear admiration. Then he rolled up the sleeve of his shirt. "What do you think? I had it done ten years ago."

Kayla wondered if it would be rude to throw Molly into the pool. However, when the woman traced a finger over James's bicep, Kayla determined it would not be rude at all. In fact, it would be quite fun.

"Hey, mom," Sam said, breaking Kayla from her thoughts.

Kayla turned to see Sam and Emma walking up. "Is everything okay?" she asked.

"It's great," Sam replied, her smile wider than Kayla had seen in a very long time. "Thank you." She gave Kayla a hug, which only intensified how happy Kayla was that her daughter was once again the girl she remembered.

When the girls leaned down to grab drinks from the cooler, she turned to James and Molly, who were talking as if they had known each other for years. A knot formed in the pit of her stomach. "Hey, are you ready to go swimming?" she asked Sam, although she would have preferred to stay and monitor the pair standing before her in a much too friendly manner.

"Not yet," Sam replied. "But come and hang out with me."

Kayla bit at her lip. What was wrong with her? James was a grown man, and it was not as if they were an item or something. Plus, what was wrong with him talking to a woman who clearly had similar interests? She placed a hand on James's arm. "I'll be back in a bit," she said, secretly hoping he would stop her from going.

"Take your time," Molly said. "I'll keep him busy!"

"I'm sure you will," Kayla mumbled under her breath as she forced the fakest smile she had ever done in her life. She walked over to where Sam and several of her friends stood talking, but she could not help but glance over at the pair who now seemed to be deep in conversation.

"This party's great, Kayla," Emma said.

Kayla smiled at the girl. She had meant what she said about enjoying having Emma over. "I'm glad you're having a good time. So, do you have any plans for the summer?"

Emma shot Sam a glance, and Sam nodded as if in encouragement. Kayla wondered what the two were up to. "Well," Emma said, her tone obviously nervous, "Sam told me she would be working at the diner, and I was wondering if I could work there, too."

Kayla considered the two girls carefully. Having them at the diner would allow her to keep an eye on them, even if it was only once a week. In all honesty, she could not afford to hire on anyone else, but it would be nice to give the girl a chance to earn a bit of spending money, as well as gain some work ethic.

"How about you come in on Saturdays with Sam. You can start next week, if you'd like. It's going to be early, though. Do you think you can handle it?"

Emma squealed. "Yes, I can!"

"See, I told you my mom's cool," Sam said, and Kayla felt like crying tears of happiness. Sam finally thought she was cool. "Okay, time for us to swim. Are you coming, mom?"

Kayla shook her head. "Not today," she replied. "But you two have fun."

The girls walked over to the pool where at least eight teens were already splashing and horse playing in the water. Two of them were boys, but thankfully, Curtis, one of the two boys' father, was there supervising. Kayla walked over to the man and thanked him for chaperoning; it certainly was not something many parents wished to do.

She made her rounds, stopping periodically to greet some of Sam's classmates or the parents who had come, when she heard a loud laugh that made her turn. Both Molly and James were at the grill, and Susan had joined them. The aroma of hamburgers and hot dogs cooking wafted through the air, but it was not the food that piqued her attention. Her jealousy spiked once more when she saw Molly lay her hand on James's arm as she laughed at something he had said, and Kayla wondered how Susan could betray her by encouraging such behavior. She let out a sigh; she knew she was acting immature. She walked over and joined the trio.

"Hey," James said. "I hope you don't mind, but Susan suggested I start cooking up the food."

"Not at all," Kayla said. She shot Molly a smile. "I'm sure you want to sit down and relax. Can I get you something to drink?"

"Thanks, but no," the woman replied as she raised the can Kayla had not noticed she carried. "I'm cool here. I've already made some new friends."

Kayla hoped the daggers coming from her eyes were noticeable. They must have been because Susan pulled Kayla aside as she said, "You two cook. I need to help Kayla get the rest of the food set up."

Kayla winced from the pressure Susan had placed on her elbow as the woman practically dragged Kayla inside.

"Okay, what's wrong," Susan demanded once they were in the kitchen.

"Nothing." Kayla avoided looking at her friend as she placed all of her attention on the buns that she was placing in her arms.

"Kayla, I've known you too long," Susan said, taking the package out of her arms and returning it to the counter. "Have I done something to upset you? I'm sorry about my jokes toward James. I don't mean anything by it."

Kayla regarded her best friend and let out a heavy sigh. She knew Susan was harmless and would never betray her, but she was not so sure about that other woman. However, how could she explain an emotion that she so rarely felt; it was a surprise when it reared its ugly head? "I know," she assured Susan. "It's kind of embarrassing to admit."

"What?" Then realization crossed Susan's face. "You're jealous, aren't you?"

Kayla nodded. "I shouldn't be," she said, her stomach rolling at the thought. "I mean, we're just dating. It's not like it's serious or anything. He's not my boyfriend. I can't stop him from talking to someone else, I know that. But she seems really intent on hitting on him."

Susan glanced around as if to make sure no one could hear her. "Look, he's a good-looking man," she said in a low voice, even though they were alone. "To be honest, I think she's flirting with him pretty hardcore. But it doesn't matter."

Kayla stared at her in disbelief. "But it does to me," she said, but then she cringed. She sounded like one of the teenagers out back.

Susan laughed and gave her a hug. "Honey, it's obvious he only has eyes for you. No woman is going to change that."

"Are you sure?" Kayla asked skeptically.

"Of course I'm sure," she said. Then she began loading the packages of buns into Kayla's arms. "Now, come on, let's go eat."

Kayla considered Susan's words and realized that jealousy was not going to get her anywhere. And if Susan could tell James would not be distracted by another woman, then she had to believe that everything was going to be fine.

***

Susan was wrong. No, she was not just wrong, she was way off. Kayla peeked through the blinds onto the back patio. It was just past midnight and all of Sam's classmates and their parents had gone home hours ago—well, most of them. Susan was asleep in the guest bedroom and Emma and Sam were upstairs. But outside, under one of the outdoor lights, stood James and Molly. Kayla wiped at her eyes as she watched James take Molly's hands in his own in an almost loving manner.

Kayla wondered if she and James were just too opposite for each other, if she was too plain. Molly had a great look, a free rocker spirit. Kayla glanced down at her plain, suburbia outfit and sighed. Though it had never been something she had considered in the past, perhaps she should get a tattoo. Maybe a new look; she could cut her hair short or wear 'hipper' clothes. Anything to keep James's attention.

However, the idea dissipated as Molly put her arms around James and the two embraced. Even from this distance, Kayla could see James say something in Molly's ear. Maybe he was asking her out on a date or he was offering to take her out on his motorcycle, something Kayla still had not done with him.

The embrace broke, and then Molly walked toward the back door.

Kayla rushed to the kitchen and began scrubbing at the counter as if it had a stain she was struggling to remove. She only took a moment to glance up when the door opened and Molly entered.

Molly's face was beaming and her eyes were alight. Kayla knew that look all too well; it was a look James could give a woman, for she herself had felt it.

"Hey," Molly said, "do you need any help?"

Kayla kept a rein on the sneer that attempted to cross her lips. How dare this woman come to her home and steal away the man she was dating? "No," she replied curtly.

"Okay…" She shifted her stance and then yawned. "I guess I'll head upstairs. Thank you again for opening your home to me. I'm exhausted, but I was wondering if we could talk tomorrow."

Kayla bit at her lip. She could imagine how that conversation would go. It would be the 'I like James and I hope you don't mind if I go out with him' chat.

"Sure," Kayla said as she pushed past Molly to put away a container in the fridge, hoping the woman would take the hint.

She did. "Um, okay. Well, goodnight." She headed upstairs to the room Kayla had shown her earlier. Now she wished she had not offered to have the woman stay.

Kayla's stomach sat heavy in her belly. Now that Molly was gone, it was time to confront James. It was going to be difficult, but as she headed outside where he was still standing staring out toward the lake, a thought came to her. She might not have lost him just yet.

"Hey there," she said as she walked up to James. "I have great news." James stood up and smiled, but she added, "No, please, sit." She took a chair next to him.

"I've got something to tell you, too," he said. "But you'll have to brace yourself." His face was very serious and Kayla's heart skipped a beat. If she didn't implement her plan now, it would be too late.

"Me first!" she said before she lost her nerve. She grabbed his hand. "I'm going to Denver next week to get my tattoos done."

He screwed up his face in confusion. "Tattoos? You're getting inked?"

"Yes," she said firmly, though her nerves were making it difficult to breathe. "I've been wanting to get both my arms done, full length."

He gave her a bewildered look. "You mean full sleeve?"

She laughed, hoping he would not hear her uneasiness. If this plan was to work, he needed to believe she was all in on making these changes.

"Exactly," she replied. "And then I've been thinking about a new look. What do you think? Full leather? Maybe some more piercings?" She let go of his hand and pulled her hair back. "Four on each ear. Then, I need some rings, tough looking ones."

He shook his head. She was surprised to see that his eyebrows were almost up to his hairline. "Really? You want to do that?"

"Yes. I've been wanting to for quite some time," she said. She felt bad for lying, but her desire of making sure Molly did not win him was much too strong.

Still holding her hand, he shook his head. "Kayla, can I ask you something? And will you be honest with me?" She nodded. "Does this fascination with getting tats and a new look have anything to do with Molly?"

Kayla bit at her lip. "I can be like her, if that's what you want. I can change. I know I'm not as edgy…"

"I don't think you understand."

"No, I do understand. I'm far too different from you. I know I must be pretty boring, but we can change that. So, let's go to Denver, get my tattoos and new clothes." She looked at him pleadingly. "I understand if you want to date her, but give me a chance, because I think I'm worth keeping."

She struggled to keep her emotions under control, and he reached over and put his arms around her.

"I'm not dating her, nor do I want to," he whispered in her ear.

She sat back in her chair. "But you two were talking all day, and then…well, I didn't mean to, but I kind of spied on you a bit ago. I saw you holding hands…and then hugging."

James laughed and then pushed her hair back behind her ear. "Oh, Kayla. Wow, you are so awesome," he said. Somehow, that made her feel more like she was acting childish.

"What do you mean?" she asked, feeling even more confused.

He reached over and handed her a napkin, which she used to dab at her eyes. "Yes, we talked a lot today, and yes, we have a lot in common in terms of music and body art.

But what you saw was not two people holding hands because they liked each other." He gazed at her, and she found herself holding her breath. "I prayed for her."

"You what?" Kayla asked, her mind scrambling to comprehend what he had just told her.

"I prayed for her," he repeated. "She's never been to church, and going through her recent divorce, I told her that church could be what she needed. Then I offered to pray for her. Afterward she said she felt better and would be coming this Sunday."

Kayla let out a deep sigh, so embarrassed she could barely remain in her seat. What she really wanted to do was run into the darkness beyond the lights of the house and hide. She had just made a total fool of herself with her fast judgment, making assumptions and then allowing those assumptions to run amok. This was not like her. How could she have been so wrong?

"I'm so sorry," she whispered. "Oh man, I was so rude to her a little bit ago. She said she wanted to talk tomorrow..." Her voice trailed off. How could she even articulate how awful she felt right now?

"I told her about the women's meeting you guys have," he said. "She was interested in that and wanted to talk to you about it."

All Kayla could do was cover her face with her hands. "I am so sorry," she said, her voice muffled. Then she looked up at him. "Can you ever forgive me?"

His smile was so kind, Kayla wondered if it was real. "Of course I can," he said. He pulled her in for a hug, and in that hug, she felt relief wash over her. She also felt safe, and that was the greatest feeling in the world.

"There's one thing I wanted to share," she said when the hug ended. "I'm sorry for being jealous..."

His voice was gentle as he placed his fingers under her chin. "I want us to take our time," he said. "Even though you can do what you please, date whoever you want, I'm not interested in dating anyone else. I just thought you should know."

Kayla wondered if her grin was as goofy as it felt.

"Look, I better get going," he said, "You and Sam have plans tomorrow, right?" He released her chin, much to her disappointment. What had she expected? That he would kiss her right after her crazy rant about Molly?

"We do," Kayla replied. "But I'll see you at church on Sunday, right?"

He smiled. "You got it."

She walked him to the front door where he gave her another quick hug. After wishing him a good night, she closed the door and headed upstairs, happy for her, happy for Molly and Emma, and most importantly, happy that God had taught her another important lesson about humility and trust.

Chapter Thirteen

James paced back and forth across the living room of his trailer. Kayla would be arriving at any moment, and it was her first time to visit. He was not ashamed, per se, of where he lived, but it was nowhere near as nice as her house.

His furniture consisted of an old couch, a single mismatched and beaten up chair and a heavy coffee table refurbished from an old pallet. Everything he owned he had purchased at the thrift store in town, and it was easy to tell it was second-hand. The nicer items, even at the thrift store, were outside his budget, so he had to resign himself to the less attractive of the lot. Usually, it would not have bothered him, but he could not help but feel just a tad uncomfortable.

The crunch of tires pulling up had him peeking out between the blinds. It was just past seven, and Kayla was stepping out of her truck. Though he had seen her at work throughout the week, they had not spent any time together since Sam's party last week, and his stomach felt as if it were stuffed with bricks as he opened the door and stepped out onto the stoop.

"Hey, you," she said as she walked up to him.

James sucked in his breath. She was wearing a purple shirt and a pair of shorts, and though neither was revealing or immodest, he could not help but notice that the woman had some legs on her. He quickly moved his eyes back up to her face, which was another mistake. Her red hair flowed behind her as she walked and the sun highlighted the radiance of her face. Surely there was no woman on earth as beautiful as her, and the smile she gave him only confirmed it.

"Hey," he was able to choke out as he opened the screen door for her. "Come on in." She walked past him and they both stood in the living room. "So, this's it. It's not much, but it's home."

"I like it already," she said as she turned toward him. "It feels cozy and that couch looks inviting."

He crunched his brow. "Really?"

"Yes!" she said excitedly. Then she turned and gasped. "Oh, I love your kitchen. I love the layout." She walked past him and ran her hands along the countertop, making herself right at home, which he loved. She opened several cabinet doors, commenting on various items she found inside. "Not bad. You seem to shop pretty well. I'm impressed."

James felt like a teenager as he stumbled over his own tongue. "Thanks," he finally got out. "So, dinner's almost ready." He nodded at the pot on the stove. "Are you hungry?"

She nodded. "I'm starving." She glanced around. "Should I sit?" she asked, motioning to the card table and two plastic patio chairs that made up his dining set.

"No, ma'am," he replied regally. "Follow me." He led her back into the living room and motioned to the couch. She took a seat, clearly trying to hide her confusion. He reached behind the couch and pulled out two metal TV trays with large red flowers reminiscent of the 1960s.

"Oh, fancy," she said with a laugh.

"You have no idea," he said. "I figure dinner and a movie and then a surprise afterward." He headed back to the kitchen, leaving her staring after him.

When he returned, he was balancing a tray he had borrowed from the diner in one hand and a dishtowel draped over his arm.

"Oh, James! I love it!" Kayla said. On the tray were two glasses of purple Kool-Aid and their dinner.

"Here you are, My Lady," he said in a formal tone as he set a plate and glass on her tray. "Mac 'n cheese with chopped up hot dogs. And yes, I did splurge. They are all-beef."

The sound of her laugh was hypnotizing, and he had to force himself to move over to his tray and set his food down. He turned on the TV and set up a DVD and then paused it.

"I'll say a prayer," he said, taking her hand in his. He thanked the Lord for their dinner and then started the movie.

When the title appeared, Kayla gasped. "*Roller Derby Mayhem Three*! You have no idea how much I love this one!"

This brought on a bout of laughter. The night was going just as he had planned. "I like it, too," he replied. "I could've whipped up something classier, but if we're going to watch such a classic, nothing would have gone better than what you see before you. It's like people who pair up fine wines with certain kinds of entrees; I like to pair up certain foods with certain movies."

"Well, I have a small part in this movie, believe it or not," Kayla said as she stuck her fork in a macaroni noodle. Then she looked up, her eyes wide. "It's a secret, though. No one knows."

"No way!" he gasped. "Tell me when." She nodded and he started the movie. They ate in silence as the movie played, and James could not help but glance over at Kayla every so often. She was practically glowing, and he could barely take his eyes off her.

"Okay, here it is," she said as a specific scene appeared on the screen.

He leaned forward and watched as a man with a leather vest and a green Mohawk stood in the middle of the roller rink. Then he saw a young version of Kayla skate up, her red hair unmistakable.

"They're killing everyone!" the younger Kayla said, pointing, then skated off again.

James laughed and then turned back to her. "Wow, that was great!" he said, pausing the movie. "How did you get into that movie?"

"Brandon had shipped off and I was bored, so when I came across an ad in the paper looking for extras, I figured, why not? To be honest, I never even told him." She giggled. "It was like my secret for a long time...I don't know, just something I kept to myself."

"Thank you for sharing that with me," he said. "I won't tell a soul." He reached across and gave her hand a squeeze. They looked at each other for a moment, the world around them seeming to have stopped.

Then James came back to his senses. "Are you ready for the next surprise?" he asked as he pushed his tray away and stood.

Kayla stood up, as well. "Definitely," she replied. "But, where's the ladies' room?"

He pointed down a hallway. "The main one is having problems. Use the one in my room. Last door on the left. And yes, I did scrub the whole thing down."

She rolled her eyes. "Good to know."

James cleared the dishes and put the leftovers in containers as he waited for her to return. A couple of minutes later, Kayla came back out.

"Okay, I'm ready," she said.

"All right, follow me."

They headed outside. A few clouds promised rain, which thankfully made it cooler than he thought it would be as they walked down the street.

"You know," Kayla said, "we still haven't gone out on your bike. It makes me wonder if you don't want to take me." She gave him a wink, which eased the sudden blast of worry that tried to overtake him.

"I do," he replied. "How about next Friday? Carl's running my shift again, so let's do it then."

"Deal," she said as they made a left.

Walking up to a small park in the middle of the trailer court, he stopped and turned toward her. "This is it," he said. "Part two of our date."

She laughed. "I love it. What are we going to do first?"

"Lady's choice."

Kayla studied the playground. "The seesaw's tempting, but I think the swings are calling my name," she said.

They walked over and each sat on one.

Pushing his legs out he quickly gained speed.

"Hey, no fair!" she said, pumping her legs even harder to gain more momentum. They both laughed as the old swing set groaned under their weight.

"I think you are going higher than me," he said.

"Think?" she said. "Buddy, I'm flying past you." Then she let out a scream as the legs on one side of the swing set lifted a few inches in the air.

James laughed so hard, tears ran down his face as she pushed her feet into the sand beneath her, making her swing come to a complete stop as he allowed his to slow on its own.

"That was great," she said. Thunder rumbled in the distance. "As a matter of fact, this has been the best date ever."

"I'm glad," he said with a smile. "I thought keeping it simple would work best. I'm sorry I don't have a nice home…"

She shot him a stern look. "James, your home's great. And I hope you know, I'm blessed for having my house and its location. I don't look down on anyone or think I'm better for what I have."

"I know that," he said. "It's just my insecurity. Sorry,"

Her voice softened. "There's no need to be sorry. You're fine. My house's too big for just Sam and me. Brandon and I had talked about having another child, but then…"

James glanced over and saw the stricken look on her face. He stood and pulled her into his arms. "I'm so sorry," he said. "I didn't mean to bring up bad memories."

"No, it's okay. It's not your fault. But that was the reason for the house; we wanted to have more kids, but that didn't happen." She gazed up at him, her head tilted. "Did you ever want to have kids?"

He pushed her away lightly as he pushed away the memories that threatened to overtake him.

"James?" she asked, her voice concerned.

"It's hard to talk about, but…"

She took his hands in hers. "You don't have to tell me," she said quietly.

However, he found he wanted to tell her, that he needed to tell her. Maybe not all of it, but just a little. "Bethany was five years old, the cutest thing you would ever see," he said, his voice choked as he spoke. "I was working in the garage and Vicki was on her phone when I heard the horn of a car followed by the brakes and squealing tires." He stared down at the ground and took a deep breath to calm his nerves.

"Oh, James," Kayla said, "I had no idea. I'm so sorry." She pulled him into her arms, and for the first time in a long time, the sadness overwhelmed him. Her hold was comforting and loving and he was thankful for it.

A few moments later, he pulled himself from her embrace. "There's a lot more to it," he said, feeling a little better for having shared. "I hope you can understand, but I just can't tell you right now."

"It's fine," she assured him. "Tell me what you want when you need to."

A raindrop landed on her nose and he brushed it away. As he looked into her eyes, he knew she told him the truth; he could tell her anything, and no matter where their relationship ended up, she would be a rock he could lean on.

"You know, I'm glad I told you. We learned more about each other and for that, I'm thankful. I like you a lot, Kayla. I hope you know that."

"I like you, too," she said and gave him another hug.

When the hug broke and he looked into her eyes, he could not imagine being anywhere else at this very moment. Though they were friends, it was apparent it was becoming more, something he was more than grateful for. And hand in hand, as the rain fell around them, they hurried back to his trailer.

Chapter Fourteen

The aroma of bacon filled James's nostrils as he plated it and set the plate on the counter. "Order up!" he called out.

Betty thanked him as she took away the plate to deliver it to whomever the hungry customer was. James glanced through the opening between the kitchen and the service area and noted that Emma was busy rolling her silverware for the dinner shift, but Sam was nowhere to be seen. She had probably snuck out the front again to use her phone.

He sighed. He had promised Kayla he would keep an eye on the girls while she made a quick run to the bank, but he was so busy, the best he could do was peek out every once in a while to see that they were both working.

"Hey, Betty," he said, walking out of the kitchen and wiping his hands on his apron as his eyes scanned the dining room, hoping that the girl had simply chosen a booth to work at.

"Hey, stud," Betty replied, "you forgot the hash browns."

"Ah, sorry," he said with a laugh. He had been so focused on checking on Sam that he had left the hash browns on the grill. Rushing back to the kitchen, he was happy to see they had not burned. After plating the food, he slid it across the counter.

Deborah walked in as he finished scraping down the grill. A heavyset woman with a friendly demeanor, she greeted him with the same exuberance she had since he first started working a few months ago.

"How ya holding up, slim?" she asked, and James laughed. "What's so funny?" She put her apron on as James shook his head.

"I get called slim, muscles, stud, but no one ever calls me James around here."

"Don't know what to tell you, cowboy," Deborah said as she gave him a wink, which made them both chuckle. "Now, get out of my kitchen and enjoy the rest of the day."

He did not need to be told twice. "You got it," he said. He headed back to the break room, undoing his apron as he walked, and went to toss it in the laundry basket, which was full. Rather than leaving it for someone else to take care of, he threw his apron on top of the rest, headed back to the washing machine and emptied the basket into it.

Once the machine whirred to life, he headed back up front where it was still semi-busy, thanks to the tourist season being in full swing.

Emma looked over as he walked up. "Uh...hey, James," she said nervously. She was a sweet girl, but something definitely had her worried.

"Hey," he replied. "Do you know where Sam is? I haven't seen her for a while."

Emma bit her lip and concentrated on the silverware she was currently wrapping in a napkin as if the spoon might jump out of her hand and run away. "I like motorcycles," she blurted out without looking at him.

"That's great, Emma, and we can talk about it sometime, but I need to know where Sam is." Did she think he was born yesterday? It was amazing how often teens forgot that adults were once their age.

She set the still unrolled silverware in the tub, took a deep breath, and then turned toward him. "The problem is if I tell, Sam said she would get mad at me," Emma said, her voice trembling. "I don't want to lose her friendship."

"What if I guessed where she is? That way, you're not telling me and I just happen to find her."

Emma considered this for a few moments and then picked up the silverware once again, returning to her work as she whispered, "The arcade."

James thanked her and then headed outside.

Elm Street was packed with people trying to find empty spaces to park and the sidewalks were full of people meandering from shop to shop, most more than likely simply enjoying the vacation they had waited for all year. At this moment, James wished he were off somewhere else relaxing rather than traipsing after a teenage girl.

He did a light jog across the street, walked into the arcade and spotted Sam in a far back corner—and she was not alone. A boy had his arms wrapped tightly around her and the two were engaged in a very serious kiss.

"Hey, Sam," James said as if she were simply standing there looking at one of the games, "I think it's time for you to get back to work."

She jumped back from the boy in surprise, but it did not take long for a scowl to cross her face. The young man with her had a look James had seen all too often throughout his life—cocky and angry with a stance that said he was ready to start a fight. Though James tried not to judge people by their appearance, he knew people, and he could tell immediately that this boy was bad news.

Sam glared at James. "Thanks, but you're not my dad," she snapped.

The young man with Sam laughed. "Who is he?" he asked as he shot James a scowl that rivaled Sam's.

She snorted. "Some loser my mom's dating," she replied, her lip curling and her eyes daring James to say something back. "Come on, Billy." She pulled the boy by the arm as she moved to walk away.

James had promised to keep an eye on Sam and he knew Kayla would not approve of her hanging out with some boy Sam had not even bothered to introduce to her mother, which he knew for a fact she had not since Kayla had yet to mention him, so he stepped in front of Sam, blocking her way.

Her face reddened significantly and her scowl deepened. "What?"

"It's time to get back to work," he replied levelly. He would not allow her to get the best of him. He was the adult and he would do what he could to remain as such.

Billy shoved himself in front of James. "Hey, man, why don't you back up?" he huffed.

Although James had sworn off violence years ago, he knew how to turn the intimidation up a notch, just enough to get his point across without actually becoming violent. "I'll tell you what, son, you make me back up." He gave Billy a level, but menacing, glare. "Or we can go out back and settle this, man to man?"

Billy paled as the realization set in. He turned to Sam, his voice shaky, although his attempt to cover it was noteworthy. "I better go," he said. "I'll see you around sometime." With that, he ran through the maze of machines toward the front doors and was soon lost amongst crowds of families having a good time.

Sam shot daggers at James. "You had no right to talk to him that way!" she shouted. A few people turned to stare, but either she did not notice or did not care.

"That boy is bad news," James said. "Besides, your mom wants you at the diner. You're not supposed to be out."

She shook her head angrily and he could see the look in her eyes. However, he recognized that it was not a hurt for the situation at that moment, but rather something deep down inside, something she tried to keep well-hidden.

"I can make my own decisions," she said in a low voice, her face pinched with rage. "You may want to take over mom's life, but you're not taking over mine." She pushed past him and followed the same route that Billy had just taken. James shook his head as he followed behind her, but she stopped and spun around to face him. "You don't have to follow me."

He shrugged and she grunted in anger, but he only smiled. Apparently, she did not appreciate his positive outlook on life because she groaned and then stomped out of the store.

She stopped again when they got to the corner of the park. "Seriously, you don't have to follow me. Can't you see I'm going?"

"I can see that," he said but refused to elaborate. He could have said 'Yes, but I have to go back to the diner and get my stuff' or something like that, but in all honesty, he did not have to explain himself.

Plus, it would only continue the battle, and he was not going to allow her to bait him.

"Look, I don't like you. Can't you see that?"

He shrugged again. "You've made that perfectly clear," he replied, still maintaining a level tone.

"Then why do you care what I do?

"Because I care about you and your mom."

Her laugh lacked even the smallest bit of humor as she reached in and pulled out a pack of cigarettes. James knew she was testing him and he decided that, for the moment, he would say nothing. He suppressed a laugh as she tried to light a cigarette and then finally managed to get it lit. It told him she did not have as much experience with smoking as she tried to portray to him.

"So, have you been smoking long?" he asked nonchalantly.

She shrugged. "About two months," she replied. She took a drag and instantly began to cough. "I like it."

"I used to smoke, too, you know?"

She raised her eyebrows at him. "Really?"

"Yep, but the stink it does to your clothes isn't worth it. Plus, it only takes about six months for your teeth to go yellow." He was not going to give her the typical lecture about lung cancer and emphysema most adults gave kids because it rarely convinced them to stop. No, he needed to hit her where it would matter now. "I heard some goth kids are into it, among others."

She gave him an indignant look. "I'm definitely not goth," she snapped.

He decided to roll with it. "That's surprising," he replied as he leaned against a post. "I figured you as that...or what we called a 'follower'." He kept his gaze on the playground on the opposite side of the park.

"What do you mean?"

"Oh, you know, the kids who try to look cool, rebel against their parents. You can spot them a mile away. They smoke or find some kid to date who they think is a rebel but then come to find out they're not a rebel. In all reality, they are hurting as much as everyone else."

She dropped the cigarette and ground it into the sidewalk. "I'm not hurt," she said. "And Billy, well, he's in trouble a lot, but I don't really like him."

James turned to look at Sam. "Look, I don't plan on telling you what to do. It's not my place. But can I at least buy you some teeth whitener? I would feel bad if I didn't do at least that."

She walked over and deposited the cigarette butt, followed by the remainder of the pack, into a nearby trash can, which surprised James. Rebellious teens just did not clean up after themselves, especially in public. When she returned, she gave him a cold stare. "I'm done with that," she said. "I'm not a follower. I'm a leader." She gave James a single nod.

"I thought you were strong, but I wasn't sure," he said, giving her a surprised look.

When she smiled, for some reason he was reminded of his daughter, who would have been a teenager if she were still alive. He would have loved to give Sam a hug and tell her life was rough but things would get better, but he knew it was much too early at this point. Perhaps one day she would accept him as a part of her life, but right now, he had to stand back and do what he could.

"Look, I'm going inside," she said. "But can I ask a favor?"

"Sure, what is it?"

"Don't tell mom about the smokes or Billy, please?"

He let out a heavy sigh as if contemplating his decision. Granted he did wonder if keeping the information from Kayla was wise, but he had to do something to show he was willing to trust Sam. Finally, he said,

"I'll tell you what. If I tell her but I promise she won't come down hard on you, and you promise you're done smoking and with Billy, then we have a deal." He offered his hand.

She hesitated but then shook his hand. "Deal."

"Good," he replied, relieved he would not have to keep information from Kayla. "Remember, a handshake is your word and bond. Break that bond, and then your word is no good."

She nodded and they walked across the street to the diner. Sam went inside, but James stayed outside. What had happened finally hit him and he needed some time to come down from the adrenaline rush.

When he turned, Kayla came walking up. "Hey, what's going on?" she asked. "Is everything okay?"

He smiled. "It's perfect," he replied. "Are you ready for our motorcycle ride?"

"Yes, I've been so excited," she said. "Let's go!"

James shot a glance at Sam through the diner window and was pleased to see her next to Emma stacking cups in their spots next to the drink machine. He hoped she would hold true to her word.

Chapter Fifteen

Kayla's heart thudded against her chest as she closed her eyes, her hand gripping James tightly for dear life as the motorcycle rumbled between her thighs. Though she had looked forward to going on this motorcycle ride, now that she was on it, it was scarier than she could have ever imagined.

"Hey, Kayla," James called back to her.

"Yes?"

"You're squeezing my sides pretty tight," he said with a chuckle. "Let me at least reverse out of this spot before you start ripping pieces of me off my body."

She could not help but laugh as the bike rolled backward out of the parking space and then a moment later began to move forward. "This is so exciting and scary!" she said as the bike picked up speed and moved past the shops on Elm Street. "How fast are we going? Thirty? Forty?"

"Umm…seven," he said, and they both laughed. They came up to the only stop light in town, which was red. "All right, just hold on tight and you'll be just fine."

"Do you mind if I put my arms around you?" Kayla asked, worried she would fall off the bike if she didn't.

"Not at all," he said.

Her arms encircled his waist and she felt her face heat up as her hands connected in front of him. It wasn't that she had not admired his physique before, but with her arms around him, it was a whole different experience. Just being against him like this, though maybe a little intimate, felt great. She felt protected, as though nothing in the world could hurt her again.

"Here we go."

The bike moved forward, and glancing behind her, she saw downtown fade from view. Turning to face forward again, she felt the greatest exhilaration: freedom. As the bike picked up speed, the sun's rays cast light on them, the rolling hills of green on each side became a blur, and she laid her head against his back. The fear of being on the bike was gone; she knew James would keep her safe and she let out a small sigh, wondering what it would be like to hold him forever.

The bike started slowing down, and she lifted her head and saw that they were approaching the road to her neighborhood.

"So, where do you plan on taking me? Home?" she shouted, trying to be heard over the thunder of the motorcycle.

"Nope," he replied just as loudly. "The lake. I still haven't been there yet."

She lifted herself up a bit to say something in his ear to be sure he heard her, but she was jogged when they hit a bump and her lips brushed his earlobe. His body trembled in her arms and she thought she would die from embarrassment.

"I'm so sorry!" she said, wondering if she should just walk home from here. "It was an accident."

"Sure it was," he said with a laugh. "I know your type." That was what she adored about him. He could take any situation and make it funny. She wondered how he never seemed stressed or let anything bother him. He was fascinating in so many ways.

They passed her house and then took the dirt road that led to the lake. Though the road was pretty smooth, there were a few odd bumps, and she found it a great excuse to hold him even tighter. The small parking area was a graveled lot that some of the other homeowners would use to launch their boats from.

The bike finally came to a stop, James turned off the motorcycle, and Kayla felt a residual vibrating feeling that continued in her legs.

"Well? How was it?"

"I've never felt so free," she admitted. "It was scary, yet exciting. I'm going to buy a helmet so we can go further next time."

"I'm glad you liked it," he said. "You did great."

"Thanks." She felt quite giddy.

It was quiet for a moment and then James said, "Kayla?"

She smiled. "Yes?"

"Not that I mind," he said, "because it's really nice, but is there any chance you want to let go of me? Unless you plan on kissing my ear again..."

Kayla glanced down and realized with horror that her arms were still wrapped around his waist. "I did not kiss your ear!" she said with mock indignation and a light slap to his arm, although she could not help but laugh at the same time.

"You did," he replied as he lifted his leg off the bike after she stepped off. "But if you don't want to admit it, I won't hold it against you." He gave her a wink.

She pursed her lips to show him her disgust in saying she would lie about it, but then she laughed. She reached out her hand and took his in it. It felt good to have her hand held as they walked down the wooden dock.

Once they got to the end, they stopped and looked out over the lake. The surface was smooth and reflected the mountains that sat behind it, and the sun made them squint from its brightness.

"It's so beautiful," Kayla sighed.

James turned toward her. "Yes, you are."

Kayla felt her heart rate quicken as he leaned toward her. Her arms wrapped around his neck of their own volition, but she found she could not stop them, nor did she wish to try. Their lips met and Kayla thought the world would spin out of control around her. Or perhaps it was they who were spinning. The setting was romantic, the hands that gently held her were strong, but the kiss threatened to lift her off the ground and launch her into space. Though the kiss seemed to last years, in truth, it was only seconds. Yet, it was beautiful nonetheless.

When the kiss ended, they slowly broke the embrace and James retook her hand in his. "That was great," he said, his voice soft.

"I think so, too," she replied, just as softly.

They turned to look back at the mountains, and Kayla's mind and heart raced. For so long, she had prayed for someone to come into her life, and she could see that the beginning of a relationship had indeed happened. And now, she realized that she wanted to take the next step toward developing a serious relationship, but a rope of fear held her back. James still held secrets about his past, and she knew whatever those secrets were, she could never hold them against him.

However, something was not right, something she could not place. But then again, he did lose a daughter and she could not imagine the pain he still carried about that. She was not sure she would have been able to deal with something as horrible as losing a child.

She glanced over at him and smiled. What was she worried about? He had promised that in due time he would tell her everything, and she reminded herself that she had to be patient. It was unfair of her to not allow him to find the right time to share the missing pieces of the puzzle that made up his past. As a matter of fact, maybe that was what he planned on doing today.

"What was it that you wanted to tell me earlier?" she asked.

"You know what?" he said as he stared across the lake. "Let's enjoy this moment."

She nodded and gave his hand a gentle squeeze.

It was quiet once again, and then he turned to her. "I guess I'd better get you back to the diner to pick up Sam," he said.

She sighed. What she wanted to do was stand here for another hour, or even days. However, she had responsibilities. "Actually, Emma's mom is going to drop her off at the house," she explained as they walked back to the motorcycle. "Do you want to come over for a bit and hang out?"

"I'd love to," he replied with a smile. "Are you sure you want me over?"

She laughed as she sat behind him on the bike. "Such a silly question. I actually want you over all the time." Then she felt her cheeks burn for admitting it, especially aloud.

***

James pulled the bike into the driveway, and Kayla felt her heart drop when she saw the RV parked in the spot as they pulled up. Ben and Evelyn, her former in-laws, stood in front of the house. Ben was shaking his head and Evelyn held her hand over her mouth in apparent shock. The motorcycle came to a stop and Kayla jumped off it.

"What are you doing here?" she asked as she walked up to them nervously. She had not told them yet about James and had planned to do it at some later time when—and if—things became serious.

"We're heading to Kansas City and thought we'd stop by and see how you're...doing," Evelyn said, her eyes widening even more as James approached and stood next to Kayla.

"Evelyn, Ben, I'd like you to meet my friend James."

"Nice to meet you," James said, extending his hand. Evelyn took it but released it quickly, as if he were carrying the plague. Ben also shook James's hand, and although he gave it a firm shake, his eyes narrowed at the same time. Brandon's parents had always been judgmental, something that had always bothered Kayla. It was the reason she had never told them about appearing in the B-movie.

"So, you're a biker," Ben said, though his tone was less than impressed.

"I guess you could say that," James replied with a smile. "Though I'm a cook by trade."

Kayla felt bad. There was no reason these people should act as if they did not approve, but that was how they had always been.

"Grandma, Grandpa!" Sam yelled as she came running up the drive.

Molly waved from her car where she had dropped off Sam at the end of the drive and Kayla waved back. Then she gave Sam a quick hug before the girl pulled herself away and ran to her grandparents.

"Want to come in?" Sam asked, still very excited. "Mom'll be busy, but I have time for you."

Kayla did not miss the underlining tone in Sam's voice and felt her jaw tighten a bit. But getting angry would not solve anything.

Patience, that was what she needed. There was no reason to cause a scene, especially in front of Brandon's parents.

"Of course, sweetie," Evelyn said and then shot Kayla a look that only showed reproach. "We will be inside. I'm sure your *friend* understands that family is here." She walked away and Kayla had to take a slow, deep breath to keep herself from snapping. Not only because of Sam pulling her antics but the way Evelyn made accusations without making them. She was a pro at making people she did not care much for to feel less than they were.

Turning to James she felt horrible. "I am so sorry," she said. "They had no right to talk to you that way. I should've said something."

James smiled. "It's okay," he said, clearly nonplussed. "I can handle it."

"Still," she said, letting out a frustrated sigh, "it was uncalled for."

"Look, let me head on out. I'm sure you're going to be busy for a while. I'll see you at church tomorrow?"

Kayla nodded and then took his hands in her own. "Don't forget Thursday's the Fourth. You're coming over and we're going to watch fireworks."

"And I get to barbecue?"

She loved that he could make her laugh. She stood on her tiptoes and gave him a quick peck on the cheek. "See you tomorrow," she said.

James got back onto his bike, and a moment later it rumbled to life and he drove off. Turning back to the house, Kayla took a deep breath to steel her nerves. Why were so many people against her these days? Especially her former in-laws, who should have been the most supportive. But it was her life and her home, and she was not going to be pushed around any longer.

Starting Over

Chapter Sixteen

Well, I don't know what to say," Evelyn said after Sam headed upstairs. Kayla had endured an hour of small talk with Brandon's parents, all the while wishing she could strangle Sam. However, it would have to wait until later; right now, she needed to speak to her former in-laws.

"Evelyn, James is a Christian," Kayla explained, though the fact she had to explain anything to these people rubbed her raw. She ignored Ben's snort and continued. "I'm not as naive as you believe I am, and I would just not bring any man around the house. He's a nice guy, and if you could look past the outside, you'd see he's a kind and gentle person."

Ben set his coffee mug down and gave her a stern look. "Kayla, no one believes you're naive," he said, though Kayla knew good and well they had always thought of her that way. "But let's be honest. According to Sam, this man comes into town, you hire him, and the next thing you know, he's here late at night?" He held up a hand when she went to speak. "I'm not insinuating anything, but I don't think it's appropriate that you have a man like that around our granddaughter."

It took every ounce of energy for Kayla not to explode. With great effort, she replied with as level a voice as she could muster, "What does that mean?"

Evelyn placed her hand on Ben's arm. "Darling, has it ever occurred to you that he may be a bad influence? He could get her into bad music or even drugs; you just never know."

The chair scraped across the floor as Kayla stood. "That's a horrible thing to say. He's not that type of person." Evelyn gasped and Ben shook his head. Belatedly, Kayla realized that her voice had risen to just below a shout and she sat down. How was it these people could make her so angry? She lowered her voice, but it still trembled with anger. "Seriously, he's a nice man."

Ben raised his hand. "Fair enough," he replied. "Perhaps we assumed the worst. But let's assume the best for a moment."

Kayla shot him a suspicious look. "What do you mean?"

"Let's assume that he's not putting on an act, that he's a nice guy and has the best of intentions." Kayla nodded and Ben continued. "He works as a cook at the diner, correct?"

"Yes."

"Sam said he lives in a broken-down trailer and drives a really old truck."

Kayla let out a sigh. "Yes, he does not have much financially, but that doesn't matter."

"Oh, Kayla," Evelyn said with a heavy sigh and a shake to her head. "It does. Brandon left you with a generous life insurance policy to take care of you and Sam. It was not intended for this man to have."

Kayla stared at the woman in shock. "No, Evelyn," she said, "that has nothing to do with the situation. He's not after my money."

Ben took a sip of his coffee then smiled at his wife. "Assume you two get serious, and even down the road you decide to remarry. Is his paycheck enough to cover the bills here? Can he provide for you and Sam?" Kayla felt like getting up and walking away. They were delusional. "I know you're mad at me," Ben continued, "but here are the facts. A man comes into town poorer than dirt. Before you know it, he's sweet-talking you and moving into your life. He has everything to gain by being with you. What do you gain? Nothing."

Kayla had enough. This was getting way out of hand and she was not going to stand for it any longer. "Thank you for the advice," she said evenly, "but I will continue dating whomever I want. Now, if we can change the subject, please, that would be wonderful."

Evelyn stood, her face covered in a scowl she must have been holding back for the entire discussion. "Well, I guess you have said your piece," she said in her crisp, disappointed voice, a favorite she used when talking to Kayla. "We did our best, but apparently our opinion is no longer important to this family. I think it's time we continue our trip. Brandon would be appalled at how you talked to us. Come, Ben, let's say goodbye to Sam."

Kayla closed her eyes, and when she opened them, they were gone. Grabbing her phone, she headed out back to call James.

***

After calling James and learning about what had transpired with Sam earlier today with the cigarettes, Kayla called Susan. She needed a friend to talk to, and Susan was already on her way over. But for now, it was time to deal with Sam.

Heading upstairs, Kayla felt both anger and disappointment rage through her as she approached the bedroom door. She gave it a quick knock and then entered without waiting for a response. Sam was lying propped up on her pillow on the bed, her phone in her hands.

"We need to talk," Kayla said, going to the bed and sitting down.

Sam ignored her and Kayla reached over and took the phone out of her hands.

"Seriously?"

"Yes." Setting the phone on her lap, Kayla turned to her daughter. Her raven-haired, beautiful daughter who was slowly becoming a woman. But that sweet girl she longed for was nowhere to be seen. In her place was a spoiled, vindictive child who only looked like she was maturing.

"Fine," Sam grumbled.

"So, I found out about your escapades today. Smoking again? And Billy? Seriously?"

Sam crossed her arms over her stomach. "I told James I wouldn't smoke anymore. And I'm done with Billy."

Kayla shook her head. She wanted to believe her, but somehow she could not get herself to do it. "Right. Because this is the third time you said you were done with smoking, and I'm just supposed to believe you now?"

Sam shrugged. "I shook James's hand. He said I gave my word and my bond, and I'm not some loser who's going to break that."

Though she was probably foolish for doing so, Kayla believed her. She had to trust that what she had taught her daughter before now would kick back in at some point.

"James told me he made a promise that I would not come down on you for this. So, I'll honor his request since you're going to honor yours."

She took Sam's hand in her own. "Why did you say those horrible things about James to your grandparents? What has he done to upset you so bad?"

Sam shook her head and pulled her hand away. "You wouldn't understand."

"Sam, I've tried to understand. I try to get you two to talk. He has never intruded or told you what to do. Am I not allowed to find someone in my life?" Kayla felt the sadness rise up in her. "We don't talk anymore, honey, and it breaks my heart. We were like best friends, and now we act like roommates that can't stand each other."

Sam wiped at her eyes. "I can't tell you, because you won't get it."

Kayla nodded and let out a sigh. "Would you like to go to Denver? We can still do that, you know?" Sam shook her head, and frustration welled up in Kayla. "I can cut back date night with James if you want so we can do stuff together. I miss those times." She took her daughter's hand. "Maybe after church tomorrow we can…"

"Sheesh, you don't get it," Sam snapped, pulling her hand away. "I don't care about stupid James or hanging out with you."

Tears rose in Kayla's eyes. "But why? What have I done that's so wrong?"

Sam got off the bed, headed over to her vanity table and stood with her back to Kayla. "It's not you," she said in a voice so quiet, Kayla could barely hear her. "Well, not all of it."

Kayla walked over to her daughter and rested a hand on her shoulder. "Then tell me, honey. I can't help you if I don't know what's going on." Then a thought came to her mind that made her blood run cold. "Has someone hurt you?" The thought of that scared her, but she needed to know.

Sam turned around and then shook her head. "It's church," she replied, her lip quivering, "and God. I hate going and I want nothing to do with Him anymore."

Kayla stared at her daughter in shock. "What? I don't understand."

"Don't you get it!" Sam screamed. "He could have saved dad! We prayed every day for his safety, and then what happened? He died! God killed him!" Tears were streaming down her face and Kayla could not stop the hurt she felt in her heart. After all these years, her daughter had been suffering, and she had been too busy to notice.

"Oh, honey," Kayla said as she pulled her daughter tight against her. Sam sobbed into her chest as Kayla stroked her head. "It's not like that at all."

"I don't care," Sam said, wiping at her eyes as she gave Kayla an angry push. "You can keep believing in prayer if you want, but I don't anymore. So, please, stop talking about any of it around me." She stormed past Kayla and flung herself on her bed.

Kayla walked over and knelt beside the bed, placing her hand on Sam's arm.

"Honey, we need to talk more about this."

"I don't want to," Sam said in a muffled voice. "Please, it hurts talking about it. Don't make me."

Kayla nodded her head as she stood. She could not hold back the tears that rushed down her cheeks and dripped on the bed. She brushed back Sam's hair from her face and gave her a kiss on her forehead. "I love you. I hope you know that."

It was quiet for a moment, and when Sam did not reply, a sick feeling rose in her stomach. She walked to the door and stood to stare back over at the bed. *Dear Lord, please help my daughter,* she prayed silently. Just as her hand touched the doorknob, the sweet sound of her daughter's voice came to her ears.

"Mom?"

"Yes?"

"I love you, too."

***

Kayla took a sip of her wine and then set it back down on the coffee table. Turning to Susan, she smiled. "Then she tells me she loves me," she said as both she and Susan wiped tears from their cheeks. She had told Susan everything from the motorcycle ride to the sudden appearance of Brandon's parents to Sam's confession just over an hour ago.

Susan leaned over and kissed Kayla's cheek and gave her a hug. "Honey, it's going to work out," she said. "Just you wait and see. She's making progress. It's slow, but it's progress."

"I know you're right," Kayla replied with a heavy sigh. "But it just hurts knowing she feels that way and that I didn't see it."

"That's not your fault. You've been there, but she held it in; it's not like you can read her mind. But you know, it says all things end up working together. So, this will work out in the end."

"She shocked me, as well," Kayla said. "She told me that she and James shook hands and that she was not going to break the bond she made."

"That man's something else," Susan said, the appreciation clear in her tone. "You know what I mean. He really is great."

"He is," Kayla said with a smile. She glanced over and Susan had a huge grin on her face.

"What?"

"It looks like someone's getting serious," Susan teased.

Kayla laughed. "I've been thinking about it," she admitted. "He's great for me, and I really believe he will be great for Sam, contrary to what Ben and Evelyn say." This made both of them laugh. "I've decided that on the Fourth, I'm going to ask him."

"Oh, my! Kayla's going to have an official boyfriend?" Kayla laughed as Susan raised her glass. "Congratulations," she said, and they clinked their glasses together. "So, have you kissed him?"

"Susan!" Kayla gasped in mock shock. "A lady does not talk about such things." She laughed, but Susan only glared at her. "Fine. Yes, we've kissed, by the lake earlier today." Her voice became dreamy. "The sun was on us; the breeze was just right."

Susan brought her hand to her mouth. "Oh, my Lord. You really have fallen for him, haven't you? I mean, this is really getting serious."

Kayla nodded and then glanced at the staircase behind her, making sure Sam hadn't come downstairs. "Something's there. It's not love, at least not yet." This made them both giggle like school girls. "There's more I need to know about him, of course. He's holding some things back, but I think there's a good reason. I just don't know what those reasons are. But I have faith that he'll eventually tell me everything—when he's ready."

Kayla did not tell Susan about James losing his daughter; that was not her story to tell and she did not feel right spreading gossip. There had been enough heartache for the day without bringing in more.

"Is Sam still wanting to go to my house tonight?" Susan asked. "I'm getting hungry."

Kayla laughed. "I'm sure she will. Let me go ask. I'll be right back."

She hurried up the stairs, knocked on Sam's door, and then entered. Sam was writing in a notebook, which she closed quickly when she saw Kayla.

"Hey, do you still want to go over to Susan's?"

Sam shook her head. "Mom, can I ask you something?"

"Of course, honey. You can ask me anything." Kayla walked over and sat next to her daughter.

"Are you mad at me for what I said about church and prayer?"

Kayla smiled and took her daughter's hand in her own. "I have to admit it hurts me, but no, I'm not mad at you. I want you to know that I love you no matter what you do. Even when you drive me crazy."

For the first time in a long time, Sam smiled, and it was a genuine smile. "I love you even when you drive me crazy," she said and they both laughed. "How about I stay here tonight and we grab a pizza and watch a movie?"

Kayla smiled as she stood back up. "I would love nothing more," she replied and then headed to the door. "Let me go tell Susan."

"Hey, mom?"

"Yes?"

"I'll still go to church with you. But just don't get mad if I don't listen to it all, okay?"

Kayla nodded. At least Sam was willing to do that much without a fight. "I won't, honey. And thank you for opening up to me."

Sam smiled and Kayla headed back downstairs. Progress had been slow, but for the first time in months, it was finally being made. God still answered prayers.

Chapter Seventeen

Kayla looked over the items again. There were two large blankets and a small pillow on the counter, and a cooler with the drinks and snacks in it sat on the floor. She shook her head. Something else was missing, but she could not figure out what it was.

"Mom, you got it all," Sam insisted. Then she laughed. "Besides, it's a five-minute walk back to the house."

"All right, all right," Kayla said with a sigh. Now all she needed was for James to show up and they could be on their way.

The doorbell rang and Kayla smiled. "Be right back," she said. Hurrying to the door, she opened it, and James stood there, wearing a tight dark blue shirt and a pair of jeans, looking as handsome as ever.

"Wow, you look great," he said as he looked her up and down.

Kayla blushed. "Oh, this?" she said, motioning to her outfit. Granted she had chosen the purple t-shirt with silver designs on it specifically because he had commented on how purple was his favorite color. The denim shorts were comfortable and would keep her cool in the summer heat.

"Yeah, I love it."

Kayla smiled with delight. "All right, we better get going. The fireworks start in half an hour." The plan was to watch the show and then head over to Susan's afterward.

They headed to the kitchen and Kayla was shocked when Sam greeted James.

"Hey," she said.

"Hey back. How are you?"

Sam shrugged. "Tough being a leader, I guess. I told Billy I wasn't interested anymore in him, and you know what?" James shook his head. "He said he didn't care. That he was interested in Becky Hamilton." She laughed. "Well, good luck with that."

Kayla grabbed onto the kitchen chair. Sam had not told her any of this, and though she was happy her daughter had someone to talk to, Kayla had to admit she was a little jealous James was getting through to her when she could not.

"Good for you," James replied. "Do you have a new guy lined up?"

"No," Sam said. Then she blushed. "Well, maybe Kyle, the pizza guy, but no one else." She laughed and Kayla watched as the two went back and forth like old friends. She could not help but be impressed.

She grabbed the blankets. "All right, you two, it's time to head out. Sam, help me with the cooler, please."

Sam nodded and walked toward the cooler, but James stepped in her way. "No way. I got this," he said as he leaned down and picked up the cooler as if it weighed nothing.

"You make it look so easy," Kayla said, handing Sam the blankets as they headed to the back door.

"It's because it doesn't weigh much," Sam said.

James gasped, feigning shock and then they all laughed. There was a strange, but wonderful, feeling of camaraderie, and Kayla reveled in it. For the first time in a long time, she felt relaxed.

"So, what? You're saying I can't lift much?" James said.

"Yep. Here, I'll prove it!" Sam walked over and pushed down on the cooler. James lowered it and Sam sat on top. "Okay, tough guy, show me what you got."

"Samantha Jo!" Kayla gasped in horror. "Get down off of that." She turned to James. "I'm sorry."

He laughed. "I got this, if you don't mind?"

Kayla gaped at him as she shook her head.

Then Sam burst out laughing as James lifted the cooler up with Sam on top of it. "Hey, mom, he is strong after all," she said as they began to walk toward the path that led to the lake.

"I can see that," Kayla replied. "But don't stay on too long, you might hurt his back." It was difficult to comprehend the change in the girl—no, young woman—before her, but she would take this Sam to the other any day of the week.

"I'll be fine," James assured her. "Besides, if she gets too heavy, I can just drop her." He then acted as if he was going to tip the cooler over by raising his right arm, causing the cooler to slant. Sam squealed, jumped off of it, and then walked at his side.

Kayla's heart soared. All the signs were there that this was going to be a great night. Tonight was the night she was going to bring up the possibility of a relationship with James.

Sam was coming around to him, and Kayla had strong feelings as he walked between them. Kayla kept quiet as Sam and James continued to talk and banter between each other, and when they reached the shore of the lake, she flicked out the blankets and laid them on the beach.

"Sam, would you grab us a drink, please?" Kayla asked as she and James took a seat. Sam nodded, reached in and grabbed three bottles of water and passed them out.

"Why did you pack all those drinks?" Sam asked with a laugh. "We're not going to be here that long."

"I don't know," Kayla replied. "It's kind of silly taking that big cooler and only three drinks. Besides there are snacks in there, too."

Sam shrugged and sat next to Kayla. "I love you, mom," she whispered and then gave Kayla a hug.

Kayla smiled as she held her daughter. Reaching behind Sam, she took James's hand in hers, and for the first time in a long time, she felt as though she and Sam were part of a family again.

***

The night sky was perfect for a fireworks show. Any and all clouds had stayed away, leaving a dark blanket of blackness for the sparkling splendid exhibition that had been an annual event for as long as Kayla could remember.

The grand finale erupted with the best demonstration ever seen in Hopes Crest with its massive bursts of twinkling lights made up of all the colors of the rainbow, and a few that were not a part of that spectrum. The way the bursts reflected on the smooth surface of the lake only intensified their splendor.

Kayla smiled as Sam's eyes lit up, reminding her that she was still her little girl who had always loved fireworks. She even jumped when the rattling booms echoed against the mountains.

"I must admit, that was a great show," James said when the last burst of light faded from view.

Kayla nodded. "They seem to just get better every year."

He shook his head. "Well, they'll have a hard time topping off this one."

"That's exactly what we say every year," Kayla said with a laugh.

"Oh, hey," Sam said as if something had just occurred to her, "are you coming to my birthday party?"

James's brow scrunched. "When is it?" he asked.

"July twenty-fourth."

James winked at Kayla. Then he turned back to Sam and pursed his lips as if deep in thought. "I don't know," he said as his lip curled. "It sounds kind of boring." Sam gasped, but then James quickly added, "I'm kidding. I would love to go."

They all stood up and began collecting the things they had brought down from the house.

"Great," Sam said happily. "I'll get you a list of what I want, then."

Kayla rolled her eyes. "You're terrible." But she knew Sam was teasing. Or at least she had better have been.

"Sometimes," Sam replied with a laugh. Then her phone rang and she glanced down at it. She smiled as she brought the phone up to her ear, and then she said, "Mom, can I go to Emma's?" Kayla hesitated for a moment. "Please?" Sam begged. "You can talk to Molly if you want. There won't be any boys around."

Kayla sighed. "All right," she replied. "I trust you."

"Thanks!" She walked away for a few moments and when she returned, she said, "They're on their way to pick me up. Can I run ahead and get my stuff?" She gave Kayla a beseeching look.

"Fine," Kayla said before giving her daughter a quick hug. Then Sam was running up the path back to the house. Kayla turned to James and set the folded blanket on the cooler. With the fireworks gone, the only light came from the stars and the moon, but both were bright enough to illuminate their path.

Kayla took James's hand in hers. "Sam's taken a liking to you," she said. "I still can't believe how much she's starting to change."

"Well, she's a good kid. Like I said before, it's going to be tough, but she's coming around."

"I have to admit, I'm a bit jealous she's telling you things she has yet to tell me. But as long as she's telling someone, I can live with that."

James smiled and she bit her lip. There was so much she wanted to tell him, to open her heart up.

"James, I wanted to ask something."

"Of course. You can ask me anything."

She took a deep breath to calm her shaky nerves. Why did she feel like a schoolgirl when she was with him? It was not a bad feeling, per se, but it was a bit unnerving now that she should have been old enough to handle her feelings. "The last few months spending time with you have been great. Almost magical. You see, just like you, I've been praying for someone in my life. And when you rolled up on your motorcycle, I have to admit, it wasn't what I was expecting." Then she laughed. "I didn't mean it like that!"

He laughed. "I understand what you mean," he said. "I wouldn't usually be your type? Is that fair enough?"

She nodded, glad he understood but feeling bad how the words came out.

"Hey, it's all good," he said as he looked down at her, his eyes reflecting the attraction she had been feeling for him.

"Thank you," she whispered. "I don't know why I'm finding this so hard." She felt a tear run down her cheek. "Sam thinks you're great, and so do I, and," -her heart beat against her chest so hard, she thought he had to be able to see it— "and I want to be your girlfriend." Although she had admitted to him her feelings and had opened herself up to him, she wondered if he thought she was an immature mess.

However, he smiled and gave her hands a squeeze. But when he remained silent for several more moments, panic began to set in.

"Did I say something wrong?"

"No," he replied in a low voice. "I'm sorry. Listen, I like you a lot; I really do..."

"Is it Sam?" Kayla asked, unwilling to believe that he was about ready to turn her down after all they had been through. "She's behaving now. And if I did anything wrong, please, let me know."

"Kayla, I promise it's neither of you," he assured her. "It's me."

He took a deep breath and then let it out, but all Kayla could feel was that this was what most people said when they were not really interested and wanted to let the other person off easy.

"I like you a lot. I mean, you have no idea how crazy I am for you."

She smiled. At least that made her feel a bit better.

"Seriously, you are the answer to my prayers. But I need to talk to someone first before I take this next step. If you could just give me a few days to answer, I'd appreciate it. I'm sorry, but I need it."

Kayla nodded, though this was not what she had been expecting. She had everything planned from him agreeing to them kissing under the night sky. But now, it was like he was retreating, and even though he had tried to assure her, she could not stop the growing feeling of doom that had descended upon her.

"I'm so sorry," he said. "Please bear with me. You'll understand soon."

She forced a smile. At least he had not given her an outright no. If she had to wait for as long as she had, she could wait a bit longer. "It's okay," she said, still trying to understand but trusting him nonetheless. "Hey, are you ready to head over to Susan's?" She released his hands and then grabbed the blanket.

"Sure, that sounds fine. It'll be fun hanging out with her," he said, picking up the cooler.

Kayla smiled, though her stomach was tied up in knots.

"Are you sure you're okay?" he asked, his voice concerned.

She widened her pasted-on smile. "Oh, I'm fine. Come on."

They began walking back to the house. Inside, however, she was not fine. It seemed as her prayers with Sam were being answered, while the prayers about James were not. Sometimes she wished that God would just make up His mind, but that thought made her feel guilty. Everything was in His time, and she had to trust in that, but that did not make it easy.

Chapter Eighteen

Kayla checked her phone for the hundredth time, hoping James would call. It had been two days since the wondrous fireworks display—and James's admission that he had loose ends to tie up—and Kayla struggled to keep her agitation at bay. Although they had been at the diner together earlier, she had kept to her promise that she would give him time, but she was finding it harder than she had first anticipated. He had yet to explain what was going on, and that only increased her frustration even more.

Her mind raced as she contemplated who he had to talk to before he could make a decision with regards to their relationship. Then a thought came to mind. Was there someone else? She considered Molly but quickly dismissed it. They had gone to lunch together, but Molly had not mentioned or made eyes at James, even at church, which she did attend after James invited her during the end-of-school party. Yet, what if there was someone else? There were plenty of single women in and around Hopes Crest, several who had given James interested glances, which had only increased Kayla's jealousy.

"Mom?" Sam said as she turned off the TV, breaking Kayla from her thoughts. "What's wrong?"

Kayla waved her hand as if swatting at a fly. "Oh, nothing," she replied in an attempt to hide her frustration. Sam was a child, much too young to worry about her mother's relationships, not this early on anyway.

"Mom, I thought we were working on talking more," Sam said in a much more mature voice than Kayla expected.

Kayla studied her daughter. Sam really was growing up. The changes she had made recently had been more than Kayla could have hoped for.

"You're right," Kayla said with a sigh. "Well, I was going to wait to tell you this, but I asked James about getting serious."

"You mean like boyfriend and girlfriend?" Sam asked. Kayla nodded and then waited for Sam to lose it, but instead, she gave Kayla a thoughtful smile. "I kinda figured that. I see the way you two look at each other." She tilted her head. "Do you love him?"

Kayla sighed as she brushed back her daughter's hair. "I do care for him," she replied, "but I don't know if I love him. It's kind of early for that, isn't it?"

"Didn't you say you loved dad almost immediately?"

Kayla smiled as the memories of first meeting Brandon came back to her. "I did. But this time's a little different." She debated keeping the reason James had not accepted until later when she had an answer and decided Sam did not need to know all the details. "You see, James said he needed time to think about it."

Sam leaned back heavily into the couch. "Man, that's rough. I'm sorry, mom."

"Thanks," Kayla said with an appreciative smile. "I'm surprised you're not upset."

Sam let out a sigh, and for a brief moment, Kayla saw the woman her daughter was to become. "Yeah, I kind of feel bad about it now," she replied. "I called him a loser and told some kids he was trailer trash. But he's not; he's pretty cool, and well, he got me to stop smoking."

Kayla laughed. "I guess he did," she said. "But I'm worried, to be honest." She shifted in her seat. "What if he likes someone else? Or what if he's only interested in dating and doesn't want a serious relationship? I'm not sure I can agree to simple casual dating; I'm just not the type to want that."

"I think that about Kyle," Sam said. Then her face went red. "I like him."

"I figured as much," Kayla said with a smile. "You could talk to him at church, you know? But you don't. Why is that?"

"Well, he's cute and I don't want to embarrass myself."

Kayla laughed again. Oh, to be young again. Sam snuggled up next to her and Kayla put her arm around Sam. "I'll tell you an embarrassing story about me and your dad."

"Oh, I've got to hear this," Sam said with great enthusiasm.

Kayla's mind wandered back to when she and Brandon were only seventeen. "I was in history class," she said, "and instead of listening to the teacher, I was daydreaming about your father. So, I write this love letter to him."

Sam giggled.

"I still have it upstairs; I'll have to show it to you. But anyway, I write it out and pass the note to Susan to hand over to your dad. And you know what happened?"

"No, tell me!" Sam said, turning her head toward Kayla.

"She promptly hands it to Melvin Culpepper. Now, Melvin was a sweet boy and as soon as she passed it to him, the teacher walked over and intercepted it."

"Oh, man, that's crazy!" Sam gasped and then laughed.

"It's not over yet. Mr. Bernstein walked to the front of the class and I guess he recognized my handwriting. Then he reads my love poem to the entire class. Melvin sank down in his chair, and I wanted to dig a hole and bury myself."

When she finished her story, both of them were in fits of laughter.

"Mom," Sam said when they were both able to speak again, "I think you're cool. And though you do embarrassing stuff, I think you're really pretty."

"Aww, thank you, honey."

"Honestly," Sam said as she pulled herself up to a sitting position. "Even the guys at school say you're hot." Kayla laughed as Sam shook her head. "Yeah, it's crazy. But I think James knows you're cool, too. Just let him breathe a bit."

Kayla placed her hands on her daughter's cheeks. "How did you become so smart?"

"The Internet and late night cable," Sam replied, and they both laughed.

Kayla stood up, grabbed Sam's hand and pulled her off the couch. "Tell you what. Let's head into town and hunt around the thrift store. I'll cook for us tonight and we can watch a movie. Maybe talk about you and Kyle?"

"I'd like that," Sam said. "Let me go grab my purse."

Kayla's heart beamed as Sam headed up the stairs. Their relationship seemed to be growing tenfold every day. Sam was returning to her normal self and life, in general, was going great. Looking at her phone, she let out a sigh. However, there was still no word from James.

**

James pulled his truck up outside the house of Pastor Dave. Looking at his phone he laughed. He had been putting off buying a car charger, and now his battery was dead. He threw it in the glove box, got out of the truck and headed up the driveway. As he reached up to knock on the door, the door opened and Maria let out a shriek as she ran into James.

"Sorry!" she said breathlessly. "You scared me!"

"I get that a lot," James said.

Maria gave him a quick hug. "Head on in; Dave's watching TV. I'm going to meet with someone, but I might see you later."

James nodded and headed into the house, closing the door behind him.

"Hey, baby, what's wrong?" Dave called out.

"Nothing, honey," James said and then laughed.

Dave sat up on the couch and burst out laughing. "I didn't realize you were here," he said as he stood. "Come on, have a seat."

"Thanks." James sat in a cushioned chair next to Dave and glanced at the baseball game that was playing on the TV.

"The Rockies get worse every year," Dave groaned.

"You're telling me," James replied. "Unless they get new arms in for pitching, they're going to keep wasting money on talent they don't need."

"Can't argue you with you there," Dave said and then turned off the television. "So, my friend, what can I help you with?"

James let out a deep sigh. "Well, it's Kayla," he said. "I mean, she's great, and Sam's coming along, so that part of her life is good."

"That's great. Power of prayer."

James nodded in agreement as he leaned forward and rested his elbows on his knees. "Well, on the Fourth, she asked me if I was interested in getting serious."

"And what did you say?"

"Nothing. Well, I told her I needed to talk to someone. That being you." He was thankful that, although he had only known Dave a short time, he knew he could tell him anything. And right now, he needed to tell him a lot.

"Okay. So, my first question is do you want to progress in the relationship?"

James nodded.

"Then I guess this is about your past?"

"Yes," James replied, though it was difficult for him to admit it. "I want to tell her everything but…well, you see, her in-laws, that is, her former in-laws, were in town not too long ago, and they weren't too friendly with me. Plus, Kayla told me they disapproved. In all fairness, she stood up for me and I guess they left pretty angry."

"I know Ben and Evelyn," Dave said. "Not well, mind you, but we have met a few times. I'm going to be honest with you, James." Dave placed his hands on his knees, his face serious but still kind.

"I need it."

"There are some believers out there who still hold on to the thought that they're doing their part with others' salvation. I see it all the time."

"Even in your church?"

"Oh, yeah," Dave replied. "We have members who speak as though they haven't committed any sins and are more than proud to tell you about it. I've seen people gossip about the most horrible things. My point is you can't listen to them. I know it's easier said than done, but it's exactly what you have to do."

"I appreciate that," James said, "But with Kayla…I mean, she could retreat. I don't think she would judge me, but…" He allowed the thought to hang there. He was scared, no terrified, that if Kayla knew everything, she would reject him. The thought of not seeing her again scared him more than anything.

"Kayla has a sharp mind and a great heart," Dave said. "Here's what I would do. Start off slow, talking about your former life and those you used to spend time with. Let her soak it in, ask questions, whatever she needs."

James nodded.

"Then whether it be the same day or the following week, whenever the time's right, move onto the next part. Keep going that way. Be honest, tell her everything, and being willing to answer anything. She's a great woman, but she's grown up in Hopes Crest her whole life. So, in that way she's been sheltered. Not that there's anything wrong with that, but God has let people like me and you walk a different path for a reason."

"He sure did," James said with a shake to his head. However, he was already feeling better. "I know there was a reason I went down that path."

"Me, too. But remember, we're a New Creation, all the old things have passed away. Those men we used to be are gone now. A distant memory. It's a whole new ballgame."

James looked up at the man who God had placed in his life as a guiding light. "I feel a lot better."

"Good. Keep your head up and I'll be praying for God to give you wisdom and for Kayla understanding."

James stood up and Dave did as well. "I appreciate it."

"It's what I'm here for," Dave said. "All right, I guess we can go head out and pick up that furniture for Molly."

James followed Dave outside and the two got into his truck. He would help out with the furniture delivery and then head back home and let his phone charge. Then tomorrow, he would tell Kayla everything. If she could accept his past, then the two could take a step in the right direction, into a new future. Together.

Chapter Nineteen

To say that Kayla was excited was an understatement. She was ecstatic. James had texted her the night before letting her know that he wanted to talk to her today. And judging by the smile on his face right now, she knew it was going to be good news. Susan had a doctor's appointment and Kayla was currently covering her shift until noon. James and Carl were in the back, along with Sam, showing her how to run the grill. Leaning against the entryway to the kitchen, she let out a long sigh.

Sam was laughing along with the two men, and Kayla was happy about how Sam had warmed up to James. He was a good role model, friendly, and it was something Sam definitely needed in her life. It was just past ten and it had been unusually quiet this morning. Apparently the tourists, and even most of the locals, were either skipping breakfast or having it somewhere else.

"That's it," James said to Sam. "Now, put the plate up there."

Sam nodded and set the plate up on the small counter between the kitchen and the dining room.

"Order up," Sam called out in a very professional voice and then gave James a high-five. Carl laughed as he continued to prep items for lunch, and Kayla used her finger to beckon James over. He walked over, his smile wide.

"Trying to get my daughter to do your work for the day?" she asked.

He nodded. "You bet I am. Sam's a fast learner; she may even take my job if I'm not careful."

"Yep, that's right," Sam called out.

"You know, you're something special," Kayla said, then bit at her lip. She wanted to tell him how handsome he was, or how when he smiled it made her light up, but her daughter was standing just feet away.

"That's kind of you," James replied. "And coming from a woman as beautiful as you, I consider it an honor."

"Oh, gag me with a spatula," Sam said, and they all laughed.

Kayla turned back to James and let out a sigh. "I'm excited to talk to you later. I wish Susan would get here already." She glanced at the front door as if expecting the woman to walk in at that moment.

"I'm excited, too."

The bell on the door chimed, and Kayla gave him a wink and headed back into the diner. Betty was at a corner booth talking to a couple of locals, an elderly couple named Burt and Anne, who came in once or twice a week. However, the small group walking in the door was definitely not local. Kayla felt her heart race as she looked over the group of bikers. There were about six of them, all decked out in leather. The man she assumed was the leader looked scary with his large gut and beefy arms. He had a walrus type mustache and a bald head that looked as if he shaved it regularly.

"Hey, baby, where do we sit?" he said, his voice gruff.

"How many?" Kayla asked as she tried to control the shakiness of her voice. They had not given her any indication they were hostile, and it was unfair of her to believe they were bad people just because of the way they looked. Yet, she could not seem to keep the fear at bay.

"Ten of us," the man replied. "The women are on their way."

Kayla nodded and went over to push two tables together. She smiled as she indicated the tables and went to grab menus before returning to pass them out.

The leader grinned up at her. "What's your name?"

"Kayla," she replied. "Can I get you a drink?"

"Coffee for us and a phone number for me," he said, his eyes tracing over her making her shiver.

She headed over to the coffee stand, grabbed a full pot and returned to pour them each a cup of coffee. Betty also came over with a tray of waters, which she set in front of each chair.

Regaining her composure, Kayla stood up straight. "Now, gentlemen, our specials today are…" she started to say, but the beefy man wiped at his bald head and interrupted her.

"Honey, you're something special," he said in his oily voice. "Want to come on a bike ride with me?"

"No, thank you," Kayla replied curtly. "I'm with someone. He has a bike."

"Oh? Isn't that cute?" the man said and his friends joined him in laughter.

The door chimed and Kayla turned to see a group of four more bikers enter, all of them female.

Kayla's eyes widened at the woman who led the group. She was about Kayla's age and absolutely gorgeous. The woman could have easily been a model, but why she chose to wear a top that showed off her stomach and so much bosom was beyond her. Her blond hair was braided and her blue eyes were sharp as she scanned the restaurant. She came over and sat next to Kayla's left as the other women took their seats.

"May I get you ladies some coffee?"

"Sure," the blond said.

Kayla smiled at her and then filled their cups up as the group looked over the menu. When she returned, she stood between the bald man and the blond and reminded herself that there was nothing to worry about. James rode a motorcycle, as well, and they could be Christians for all she knew. But for some reason, she highly doubted it. There was something menacing about the group that made her hair stand on end, and it bugged her that she was judging them so harshly. She did not even know them. However, the uneasy feeling would not go away.

"All right, what are we having today?" Kayla asked, ready to write their order down.

The woman looked up. "Give me the fruit plate." Her voice was curt and perhaps a bit rude, but Kayla ignored it.

She made her way down the table, moving to each person and writing down his or her order, and soon she had returned to the leader.

He smiled up at her. "How about a stack of them hotcakes, hot stuff?" he said. Then Kayla felt her heart drop to her stomach as he rubbed her lower back.

"Bull, you're scaring the cutie," the woman said.

The man laughed but left his hand on her back.

"Please remove your hand," Kayla said, trying to keep her voice from trembling.

The man winked but removed his hand, and Kayla let out a silent sigh of relief. When she went to move, however, he gripped her arm so hard it hurt.

"Why don't you come and sit on my lap, sugar?"

Kayla shook her head and went to move her arm, but his grip was so tight, she was unable to pull away.

"Let go," she said in a louder voice as fear rushed through her.

The old couple stood and Betty watched with fear etched on her face.

Then everything happened at once.

***

James closed his eyes as Kayla took the group's order. Of all the places on Earth, and on a day that was meant to be so special, why had they shown up here? Was this some kind of test of faith? Whatever it was, James wanted nothing more than to get their orders done and get them out of here.

He closed his eyes and began to pray. When he finished, he kept his head bowed. The one thing he did not want was for any of them to see him. In fact, he would go out of his way to be sure he was not seen.

However, it was not meant to be.

"James?" Sam said.

He turned toward her and was shocked to see her standing there with wide eyes and fear on her face. "That man's hurting my mom."

He glanced through the service window and rage coursed through him as he hurried out of the kitchen. Kayla looked up at him in surprise as James grabbed Bull by his vest and yanked him to a standing position.

"Hands off, Bull," James growled as he stared down at his former assistant.

The man's eyes widened and his face filled with shock as he let go of Kayla. "James?" he gasped. "That's your old lady?"

James released Bull's vest and pushed him back into the chair, which rocked precariously but did not fall.

"Look," Bull said quickly, "sorry, I had no idea. I would never have done that if I had known."

Vicki stood, her long blond hair now braided. "James," she crooned. "It's been a while."

James stared at his former girlfriend, and memories of their past together flashed in his mind. "It has," he said as he shot Kayla a quick glance. This was what he wanted to share with her today. In his time and in his own words. But that chance was slowly slipping away.

"Come outside with me, and let's talk," Vicki said. Then she turned to Kayla. "Bull won't mess with you anymore, sweetie. He's not dumb enough to cross James."

When Kayla looked at James, he nodded to let her know that it was true. "Do you mind if I take a break?" he asked, hoping she would be patient before passing judgment on him. "Carl's in back."

"No," Kayla said in a choked voice. "Go ahead." Then she hurried back to the kitchen.

James nodded at Vicki and the two headed outside. Though the sun was shining, he did not feel the brightness. He led her to the bench that sat between the diner and the bookstore.

"You're still as handsome as the day I met you," Vicki said in her typical cooing voice. She glanced around the Town Square. "How'd you end up here of all places?"

"Lots of prayer and hope," he replied.

She shook her head and laughed. "Still believe in that junk, huh?"

"It's not junk," he said, attempting to keep his voice level. "But yes, I do."

She shook her head again. "You know, I've always loved you, James. Still do. I haven't been with anyone since you." She reached her hand out to touch his face. "Maybe me showing up here today was a sign that we are meant to be."

James pulled back. "You're always going to have a place in my heart," he said, the anger of what had just happened inside gone now, replaced by a hurt he thought he'd already dealt with. "But that man you fell in love with years ago is gone. I'm different now, and I've moved on."

"With her?" Vicki asked, motioning to the restaurant.

James turned and saw Kayla refilling coffee mugs and smiled as he turned back to Vicki. "Yes, her. She's a good woman, Vicki."

She snorted. "So, you found Jesus and a local woman from a small town. Isn't that the cutest thing?" she said, doing nothing to conceal the sneer on her face. She was the same old Vicki who would go into a rage at the slightest provocation, though, James had to admit, he used to be just like her.

He went to respond but she stepped in closer to him, her hand moving to his chest. "We had something special, you and I," she said, "until that man killed our daughter." A tear ran down her face. "There's no reason we can't have it again."

"I'm with her," James said.

She moved her hand across his chest, her words overly-sweet. "Never stopped you before, did it?"

He pushed her hand away. "Again, I don't do that anymore."

She laughed, but her eyes were filled with unshed tears. "So, you can sleep around when we're together, but now you're too good for me? Is that how it works? What makes you think you're better than me?"

"I'm not better," James said. "Don't you see? The person you knew is gone. I don't want to do those things anymore; the desire is gone."

She shook her head sadly. "I'm going to go back inside. We're staying at the motel down the road for the next few days, so if you change your mind or just want to talk, you can find me there."

James nodded. Though he could not help it, his heart was breaking. Vicki was still bitter at the loss of their daughter, and he wished he could take away her pain. He knew he couldn't, but he knew someone who could. "You know, that pain, the anger inside you, there's a way to get rid of it. God can do..."

She cut him off with a sob. "I don't want to get rid of it!" she hissed. "What I want is my little girl back!" She threw her arms around him and James closed his eyes as he held her. Her pain was so great, her hurt so deep.

"You have to let it go, Vicki. Bethany's gone." He fought back tears, which thankfully did not fall, and a moment later, the embrace broke.

"Give me your number then," she said as she wiped her hand across her eyes.

He hesitated, not sure what to do.

She sighed. "Just give it to me. We can talk before we head out. Let me know more about this prayer stuff."

He nodded and then proceeded to give her his number, which she entered into her phone. "For what it's worth," she said as she gave him a weak smile, "I'm sorry it ended the way it did between us."

"I know. Me, too," he said.

She wiped at her eyes and then with a nod, headed back inside the restaurant. Carl would be able to handle their orders, and with Vicki in there, James knew Kayla would be safe.

He headed across the street and sat on a bench in the park. A couple and their young daughter arrived and soon the young girl was laughing excitedly as the man James assumed was her father pushed her on a swing. Sadness descended upon him as he thought of his past life with Vicki and Bethany. Like when they went to the park together as a family and he heard her laughter. Yet, that life, that time, was gone. A new chapter was just ahead, though getting there was becoming harder than he imagined.

Chapter Twenty

O ver a million thoughts ran through Kayla's mind as she pretended to wipe down a table by the window as she watched James speak with the woman he had called Vicki. There was no doubt that the woman was his ex-girlfriend. Why had James lied to her and said he just rode with some friends that would sometimes get into trouble, instead of the truth, that he was part of a motorcycle gang?

Though Kayla was by no means a seasoned lip reader, she could tell Vicki had just said "Love you" to him, or something that still included those words. Then Vicki's hand was on his chest. Kayla fought back anger as she wondered if Vicki was the reason James was hesitating in moving forward with their relationship. Maybe he still loved her. She was very beautiful, and with her model-like body, Kayla knew that Vicki was the type to attract the attention of many men.

However, Kayla continued to argue with herself. James cared for her, hadn't he just told her a few days ago he was interested in no one else? Kayla's stomach felt queasy as the woman put her arms around James and he held her. It was an embrace of two former lovers, and that was hard enough. But the woman was the mother of his daughter. The two had shared a bond once, and for whatever reason, it had ended. Yet another thing James would not tell her why.

Their hug finally broke, and Kayla moved the rag over the table one more time. It would be the cleanest table in the diner by now. She glanced over and saw Betty placing plates of food on the table, and Kayla was thankful Carl had rushed the order.

It helped that no one was in the restaurant, the elderly couple having walked out once everything had quieted down once again.

When Kayla looked back outside, she could not stop herself from clenching her fist as Vicki punched what Kayla assumed was James's number into her phone. Shame, anger, and sadness all rushed through her as she made a beeline for the backroom, but Sam caught her before she could make it to her office to close the door and be alone.

"Mom?" Sam asked, her face confused.

"I don't want you going out front until those people are gone. Do you understand me?"

Sam nodded. "Is everything okay?"

"It's fine," Kayla replied, trying to keep her voice light. "But they are not good people. So promise me."

Sam nodded again and Kayla hugged her daughter, fighting back tears.

"Mom, what's wrong?"

Kayla let go of Sam and smiled. When the chime on the door tinkled, she peeked out front and saw Vicki return, but she was alone.

"Everything's fine," Kayla assured her. Then she turned to Carl. "Keep an eye on Sam. I'll be right back."

"No problem," Carl said, then continued to clean the grill.

Kayla removed her apron and threw it in the corner behind the door. She'd worry about it later. As she walked through the dining room, she glanced over and saw Vicki, who shook her head when she saw Kayla. Kayla thought of a few names she would love to call that woman, but not letting her temper get to her, she closed her mouth and headed outside.

Looking to her left and right, and not seeing James, she cut diagonally heading straight to the park. Sure enough, James sat on a bench as a family of three played in the park.

"Kayla," he said, starting to stand.

She held her hand up as she walked to stand in front of him, and he returned to his seat.

"So, those are your former 'friends'?" she asked as she tried to maintain an even voice. He nodded. "It looks like a biker gang to me."

He shook his head. "I wanted to tell you but…"

Kayla cut him off. "But you didn't. And the blond, Vicki…it's pretty obvious who she is." Try as she might, she could not keep her anger under wraps, and she found her voice rising. When he nodded again, she thought she would explode. "Beautiful woman, don't you think?"

"It's not like that."

"Oh, please. I'm a woman and I think she's beautiful." She placed her hand on her hip. "Don't lie to me."

James let out a sigh. "Yes, she's very beautiful on the outside, but on the inside…"

"Is what counts?" she asked, unable to keep the mocking tone at bay. "Please. The way she looks and dresses, I can't even compare to that. Look, I get it. She's top heavy, curvy and downright gorgeous. Then you got me. Local woman at the diner without a single flair about her."

James looked up at her. "You are by far more beautiful than she is. I have no interest…"

"I saw you give her your phone number, James. I saw the look she gave you. I'm not dumb!" She once again tried to rein in on her emotions, but they were too far gone. "And then I'm finding out all these things about you that you haven't bothered to tell me. Were you the leader of that…gang?"

"I was. I worked my way up through the ranks. And Vicki…" he said, his voice trailing off.

"Yes, the woman showing her breasts off," she spat. "I can see what kind of women you like. But it doesn't matter right now because you lied to me."

"Kayla, please, you don't understand. I didn't want to lie, but with my past, I felt like I couldn't tell you."

Kayla was taken aback. "Oh, is that so? Funny, I remember telling you things about me, about my past. Secrets I held back even from my husband." She swiped a hand across her eyes in frustration.

Why did women always have to cry when they were angry? "Yet, you couldn't trust me. Wow, I really am dumb."

He stood up. "You are not dumb, not even close. Let me explain things to you. Let's go somewhere where we can be alone and I'll tell you everything."

She shook her head, rage filling her. She had been duped, lied to, and she felt sick. "No. I'm going back to get Sam and she and I are going to spend the day together." She turned to stomp away.

"Don't leave me," he called after her. "We need to talk about this."

She stopped with her back to him, her heart wishing he would turn around; yet, her mind told her to continue walking. "Next time you want to talk, don't lie to me. I'll talk to you later," she said, then hurried back to the restaurant. There was no reason to discuss anything right now, she was much too upset to listen to him try to backtrack or cover up.

The rumble of the bikes in front of the restaurant echoed through the square, and Kayla watched as Vicki backed her bike into the street beside the others. Men on the sidewalk were openly gawking at her, and she blew one man a kiss. Then the woman turned, caught sight of Kayla, smiled at her, and then puckered her lips.

Kayla straightened her back and pushed down the anger and humiliation that threatened to overtake her as she entered the restaurant. She had no idea what she was going to do about James, but for now, she just wanted to get far away from here.

***

Kayla watched as Sam swam in the pool. Though Kayla had changed into a swimsuit, she just didn't feel like swimming. Instead, she lay out, allowing the sun's rays to warm her skin, and she did what so many other women did; she compared herself to Vicki.

Although Kayla had a similar figure to the woman who had once held James's heart, she would never have dared to wear anything as revealing as Vicki did. However, even so, Kayla decided to work on her tan so it would match Vicki's bronze skin.

Then there was her hair. Kayla had never colored her hair before, but she had heard blonds had more fun.

"Hey, mom," Sam said, water dripping from her body as she got out of the pool.

"Yes?"

"Want a drink?" Sam opened the small cooler and took out a bottled water.

Kayla nodded, and a moment later, Sam handed her a bottle. Kayla thanked her with a small smile.

"So, I have a question," Sam said.

Kayla turned her head and looked at her daughter. "Okay. Shoot."

"Well, Kyle wanted to know if we could go out sometime," she said, then quickly added, "but I told him he'd have to come by and hang out here first. So, I can get your and James's opinion."

Kayla smiled. "Is that so?"

"Yes," Sam replied as if it was the most normal thing for a teenage girl to do in this day and age, and as if not long ago she thought James was the worst man in the world. "I figure he's a good guy, he goes to church and all, but, James seems to be able to spot the good ones."

Kayla sighed. That much was obvious with Vicki. He sure knew how to pick them. But with women throwing themselves at him, he could have anyone he wanted.

"Okay. So, what did you have in mind?" Kayla asked. She still hadn't told Sam about Vicki and she did not feel her daughter needed to worry about it anyway.

"Maybe he can come over Saturday?" Sam asked, her face lit up. "We could go swimming and have lunch here."

"Okay," Kayla replied. "Two conditions." She pulled herself up into a sitting position and turned toward Sam. "One, you know the rule. You can't wear that two-piece with boys around."

Sam nodded.

"Second, I know he drives, and I know you're coming up to fifteen, but at this point, if you two decide to date, no going off in his car. Understood?"

"Definitely," Sam said.

Kayla was pleasantly surprised that her daughter had not argued with her as she would have earlier; it was a nice change.

"Thanks," Sam said, leaning over and hugging Kayla, who kissed her cheek.

When the hug broke, Sam rested back against the lounge chair. "You're really pushing for a tan today, aren't you?" she said.

"I am. Oh, what do you think about me going blond?"

Sam's eyes went wide and she shook her head in disapproval. "No way. Your hair's beautiful, just like you."

"That's kind," Kayla said with a smile, "But I'm feeling kind of plain lately."

Sam let out a long sigh, sat back up, and placed her hands on her knees. "Mom, you are not plain. I know you're jealous of that woman who came into the diner today, but you shouldn't be."

Kayla forced a gasp. "Jealous? Me? No way," she said, putting her sunglasses on so her eyes could not reveal the truth.

"Uh-huh. I saw that blond woman, too."

"She was pretty, wasn't she?" Kayla felt a pang in her stomach.

"Sure," Sam replied, "but you're more beautiful. James knows that, too."

Kayla smiled at her daughter's naivety. If it were only that easy. "Sam, you saw the way that woman looked at him. And Molly, Emma's mom, just about threw herself into his arms."

Sam's cheeks reddened. "Um, yeah, about that," she said in a quiet voice. "You should probably know that was my fault."

Kayla turned her head. "What do you mean?"

Sam grimaced. "Well, that was a long time ago, when I was jealous of James." She gave Kayla a wide smile that was a bit forced. "And well, I kind of told Molly that James liked her but was too shy to say anything."

"Samantha Jo," Kayla said in surprise. "You did not, did you?"

"I did," Sam replied and then quickly added, "but I also told her later what I had done. She laughed and said that it all led up to her and Emma going to church, so she wasn't too mad."

As Kayla looked back on the situation, she could not help but laugh. Sure, she could have been angry, but it would not have changed the fact that it happened, and Sam had been making such wonderful progress, there was no sense allowing it to become something when it did not need to be.

"Well, that makes me feel better," Kayla said. "But to be honest, I'm not sure what to do about James."

"Why's that?"

Kayla looked over at her daughter. Perhaps her daughter was old enough to be told what was going on with the man; she had certainly shown great maturity in a short span of time. "Well, he lied to me," Kayla explained. "He didn't let me know he was in a motorcycle gang."

However, rather than understand, Sam's face lit up. "I know! Tell me about it! Cool, isn't it?"

Kayla shot Sam a glare. "No. I mean, it's kind of neat, but that's beside the point. He lied about it, and after I trusted him with some of my own secrets. It's like he didn't trust me enough with his to tell me about his past."

"It's probably making it worse that you're jealous, don't you think?" Sam asked.

Kayla stared at her daughter but then gave a little laugh. "Okay, I'm a little jealous of her," she said. "She was pretty; even the guys standing outside were staring at her."

"Maybe," Sam replied, "but remember, you're beautiful. I told you the guys at school talk about you. Oh, and you know Frank at the pharmacy?" Kayla nodded. Frank was about fifty and had always been nice to Kayla. "He tells me all the time. 'Your momma ever wants to date again, let me know. That's one fine woman'." Her voice mimicked Frank, and Kayla could not help but laugh. She pulled herself up and stood, Sam following suit. "Mom, just pray about it and go talk to James tomorrow. You'll feel better."

Kayla raised an eyebrow at Sam. "I thought you didn't believe in prayer anymore?"

"I don't know if I do or don't, but I've been praying lately," she said, biting at her lip.

"For what?" Kayla asked, her heart going out to her.

"To understand why dad died." Then Sam was weeping and Kayla pulled her into her arms. As she kissed her forehead, Kayla thanked God that her daughter was once again seeking Him out.

"I love you," Kayla said.

"Love you, too," Sam replied as she wiped the tears from her face. "Do you want to go for a swim before you call James?"

Kayla smiled. "I would love to."

For the next half hour, Kayla spent time in the pool with Sam. When they had tired themselves out, they went inside and watched a movie while Sam talked nonstop about Kyle. It was a wonderful time sharing in love and laughter, and later when Sam went to bed, Kayla sat by herself, her mind reviewing the events of the day. Sam was right; jealousy had fueled a lot of her anger today, but James had still lied. But despite that fact, she needed to listen so she could understand why he had.

Grabbing her phone, she sent James a text, hoping he would want to meet her tomorrow.

Chapter Twenty-One

T he road leading into Hopes Crest was deserted as Kayla drove down it on her way to see James. They had texted late into the night, and now she could not wait to talk to him. Not only did she need to apologize for her appalling behavior the previous day, but she also had something important she needed to tell him, something she had not wished to admit before but now found it difficult to ignore.

She had fallen for him.

It was unclear how it had all come about. All she knew was that it had happened so quickly, and she had not recognized it until now; in all reality, how was she to know something that was seen only in cheesy romance movies on TV would happen to her?

She had prayed this morning and then sat down with Sam to explain what she planned on telling James. Much to her shock, Sam had hugged her and said she was happy for her. One thing Kayla knew for sure was she wanted James and nothing could stand in her way.

"Even that woman," she said in a loud whisper when she saw the motorcycle leave the hotel parking lot and pull out in front of her. There she was again, the tramp on the bike. The one person who could have a hold on James. Kayla wondered where the woman was going. She also had James's number; was she planning on seeing him?

Kayla slowed down as they came to the stoplight before the Town Square and the bike made a sudden right turn. The tires squealed as Kayla yanked the wheel, and for a second she wondered if the truck would flip over. In all actuality, it would not have, but her mind was not as it should have been.

Vicki had pulled over, hopped off the bike, and shot Kayla an exaggerated wave.

"Dangit," Kayla said with a swift slap on the steering wheel. So much for tailing; her cover was blown. Her heart raced as she rolled up and allowed the truck to come to a stop behind the motorcycle.

Vicki leaned into the truck window. "Are you following me?" she asked.

"No, I, um…"

The woman laughed. "We should talk," she said. When Kayla shrugged, Vicki opened the door. "Mind if I get in?" Then she grinned. "I'm not going to hurt you."

She was already climbing in before Kayla could reply, but Kayla squeaked out a quick, "Okay," nonetheless. Then a sudden burst of courage made her say, "You know, I could hurt you." Well, maybe it was more stupidity than courage.

Vicki snorted. "Yeah, we both know that's a lie. Go on, take me somewhere so we can talk."

Kayla nodded. What else could she do? It was not like she really could take this woman on even if she wanted to.

"I guess I should introduce myself," Vicki said as Kayla made a U-turn on Mason Street and headed back toward the stoplight. "I'm Vicki."

"Kayla."

"Nice town you live in," Vicki said as she glanced around at the different buildings. "Good place to raise a family I take it?"

Kayla nodded and then turned into the school parking lot, finally stopping in front of the sports field and throwing the truck into park.

"Come on, let's go out there," Vicki said and she started walking toward the bleachers.

Kayla sat in the driver's seat for several moments before getting out of the truck. However, as she followed the crazed biker woman across a patch of grass, Kayla started questioning her own judgment. As she glanced around, she realized no one would probably hear her screams if Vicki attacked her.

However, Vicki did not jump her. Instead, she sat down on the first row of bleachers and patted the space next her. "Have a seat."

Kayla sighed and then sat down. There was no doubt in her mind what Vicki wanted to discuss.

"Do you have any kids?" Vicki asked as she turned to Kayla. Her bikini top was purple today and Kayla was certain why she had chosen it, since purple was James's favorite color. Had Kayla not done the same when she wore her purple t-shirt? At least her t-shirt was less enticing than what this woman wore.

However, Kayla was not here to discuss fashion. "I do," she replied to Vicki's question. "A daughter. She's about to turn fifteen."

Vicki nodded and turned her gaze to the field. "Me and James had one. Did he tell you that?"

"He did."

It was quiet for a moment, then Vicki turned back to Kayla. "I don't know what James told you about me, but from what I can see it wasn't much, was it?"

Kayla shook her head. "No. I mean, he mentioned you, that you two were in a relationship and had a daughter. But not much else."

"Did he tell you we were engaged?"

Kayla shook her head again, her heart thumping. "No."

Vicki laughed. She put her left hand toward Kayla, the diamond on her ring finger reflecting the sunlight. "You know, he straight up left me because I didn't want to go to church. How's that for compassion?"

"Well," Kayla said, "it's not nice, but I wonder…"

"Not nice?" Vicki asked incredulously. "You know what's not nice? Sitting at home waiting for your man to get out of prison. Listening to him talk about how he's going to marry me. Then he finds that religion and he changed."

Kayla swallowed hard. "He was in prison?"

Vicki snorted. "You say that like you can't imagine it."

"To be honest, no." Kayla tilted her head. "Why are you telling me this?" She did everything she could to hide the heartbreak she was feeling. James never mentioned he and his ex were planning on getting married.

And prison? It was like all the stuff her former in-laws had said were true, and Kayla felt more foolish for it.

"Look, I can tell you're not exactly a city girl, are you?"

Kayla shook her head. Then she was shocked as Vicki placed her hand on top of hers.

"James is a violent man," Vicki said in a quiet voice, "made from the streets. Sure, he may have found Jesus or whatever you call it, but he's still the same man. I'm not going to lie, I still love him. And I plan on getting him back."

Kayla pulled her hand back and wiped at her eyes in frustration. How she hated that she cried. "He likes me," Kayla said with a jut to her chin. "He only has eyes for me, he's told me that."

Vicki laughed and pulled out a pack of cigarettes. "He used to tell me that, too. Until I caught him with another woman. Many times." She lit her cigarette up, took a heavy drag, and then blew out a billow of smoke that rose to the sky.

Kayla stared at the woman in surprise. "Then why do you still want him?"

"Because I know what he needs, and, sweetie, you're not it. Be honest, do you think your type and his type are made for each other?

"Yes," Kayla said, though it lacked conviction. She was beginning to doubt it after hearing what this woman had to say.

Vicki looked Kayla up and down. "You know, we have similar figures," she said. "Does that not make it obvious?"

Kayla shook her head in confusion. What was she trying to say?

Vicki stood and looked down at her. "You look like me. You have a daughter. Can't you see? He's trying to relive his relationship with me through you."

"It's just a coincidence," Kayla retorted.

Vicki shrugged and took another long drag, the smoke billowing out a few moments later. "Maybe it is. Or maybe it's like I said. But think about this for a moment. You live in a great place, have a kid, life's going good. But you're lonely. Then Prince Charming comes into town."

Kayla shifted in her seat. It was as if the woman knew her.

"Slowly, piece by piece, the mask begins to fall off of him. A lie here, finding out about someone else there. Soon the illusion is gone and you're left looking at a guy who was not who you thought he was."

Kayla felt anger roll through her as she jumped up, her fist clenched as she attempted to control her voice. "I can take you back to your bike," she said. "But I'm done here." Tough woman or not, she was not going to listen to any of her rubbish any longer.

"Truth hurts, doesn't it?" Vicki said with a triumphant smile.

"You're speaking lies!" Kayla shouted, but Vicki only shrugged.

"Maybe I am. Or maybe I'm telling you things that have you second-guessing everything. A guy like James, he picks a woman like you?" She laughed. "He doesn't tell you a word about his past; in fact, he lies to you about it. But go ahead, ask him if he still cares for me, see if he denies it."

Kayla bit at her lip. She had to get out of here. "Is that all?"

"Just keep away from him," Vicki warned, though she had retained her even tone. "He needs me. I know how to satisfy him in bed...and out of it." She took a final drag off her cigarette, dropped it in the dirt, and ground it with her boot heel.

As they walked back to the truck, Kayla's mind whirled as Vicki's words sank in, bringing on panic as she wondered if James would be better off with this woman after all.

Or was she, Kayla, better off without him?

Chapter Twenty-Two

The ring glittered in the small gift box James carried. He had saved up money and bought it at the thrift store in town, and today he was going to give it to Kayla. No, it was not an engagement ring, but rather a promise ring signifying that she had nothing to worry about when it came to Vicki—or any woman for that matter.

He wanted her to know that he was serious about her and that, in fact, he had fallen in love with her. He had never thought it possible, especially so quickly with a woman like her. She was beautiful, smart, and had such a lovely heart. Yet, it had happened, and he knew she cared for him, as well.

Although they had only shared the one kiss, there was so much hunger and passion in it that their feelings were undeniable. It wasn't the kiss, however, that led him to love her; it was the connection he felt when they were together.

The gold band held a small diamond and was otherwise inexpensive, but he felt that she would appreciate it. Then maybe one day, Lord willing, he would be able to ask her to marry him. Then he would put a ring on her finger that was more fitting for a woman like her.

The crunch of tires on the gravel in front of his trailer told James that Kayla had arrived. He went to the front door, his heart so full of love and ready to tell her everything. There would be no more holding back, no vague answers. It was time to come clean so they could begin what would be a wonderful relationship.

As Kayla stepped out of the truck, however, his smile fell. Although she was as beautiful as the first time he saw her, her eyes were red, tears stained her cheeks, and anger blanketed her face.

"We need to talk," she said, her voice stern as she approached the wooden steps.

"What's wrong?"

He still held the gift box and she stood staring at it. "What's that?" she asked.

"Something for you," he replied, though he suspected now was not the time after all. "But it's for later."

She placed a hand on her hip and glared at him. "Really? A ring?" she demanded.

"Y-yes," he stammered. "For you." Why was she so angry? He opened the box and showed her the ring. What he had expected was a smile, or perhaps a sigh and an apology, but he was not prepared for what came next.

"Oh, wow, a ring," she snapped. "One of those promise ones? Like the promise you make someone you're going to marry…when you're in prison?"

James could only stand and stare at her. His worst nightmare had finally come true. This was what he had been afraid of, the reason he had not given her an answer when she asked about moving forward with their relationship. It was the sole reason he sought out Pastor Dave—because he had wanted to tell her but was unsure how.

"I can guess how you found out," he said in a low voice. "Yes, it's true; I was in prison for three years and I can explain why." He shoved the box into his pants pocket. There was clearly no reason to have it out now.

"I don't care to know," Kayla said as she scrubbed her palm over her eye. "Did you tell Vicki you were going to marry her?"

He nodded. There was no reason to lie to her.

"I see." She went quiet for a moment and then said, "Did you ever mess around with other women while you were with her?"

There it was, the proof she had spoken to Vicki. James needed to do whatever possible to put everything into perspective.

"Kayla, you have to understand…" He reached for her, but she swatted his hand away.

"No, that tells me enough," she said, her voice dangerously low. "Now, one more question. Do you still care for her?" Her green eyes bore into him. How could he explain that Vicki was the mother of his child? A woman he spent over ten years with? He did not care for her, not in the way Kayla was meaning. "As a friend," he explained. "As someone I'm concerned about, yes, I care for her. But am I in love with her? No, not at all."

"I don't believe you," Kayla snapped. "I now find I've been dating a guy who was in a biker gang, was engaged, had been caught cheating on that woman, and who went to prison?" She shook her head, her face pinched in anger. "I'm a fool."

"No, you're not a fool," he said. "Those things are all true. I just couldn't tell you. But now I can."

Her laugh was so different from the joyousness he had become accustomed to. "It doesn't matter now," she said. "It's over, James. Whatever we had, it's over." She reached into the pocket of her jeans, pulled out her keyring, and turned to leave.

"Don't say that, please," he begged. "Don't judge me because of my past." He was not a crying man, but he felt a wetness in his eyes.

"No, it's because you lied. You lied to me. I brought you into my home. Do you realize how foolish I'm going to look in front of Brandon's parents? I threw them out of my house. Over you!" She was yelling at this point. "I told them that you were not bad, but they swore up and down I was wrong." She shook her head and looked right at him. "You make me sick."

He felt like someone had just punched him in the stomach, and worry rumbled through him. Although he stood over six feet tall, he felt like he was the smallest he had ever been in his life.

"I have a no-felon policy at work for people like you," she said coldly. "I will mail you your paycheck with a two-weeks' severance. Don't come by the diner or talk to me or my daughter ever again." And with that, she walked back to the truck.

"Kayla!" he called after her. "I need that job. I'm having trouble making it as it is since I gave Carl some of my shifts."

She opened the door and glared at him through the open window. "Maybe next time you should be honest with people right up front. Goodbye, James." She got into the truck, fired it up and a moment later, sped away.

He turned and looked up at his home. He was a felon living in a rusted-out trailer. God may have forgiven him for his past, but Kayla clearly never would. Perhaps he had been naive to think that someone of her class could ever see past his faults. Now, however, all he knew was, just like that, the door he thought his prayers had opened, was now closed.

***

When Kayla arrived home, she turned off the truck and sat staring up at her house. She could not stop the tears that burned down her face and her eyes itched from their flow. Her heart was broken and she wanted nothing more than to fill a glass with wine and drink her sorrows away.

She got out and took each step to her front porch as if it were a mountain, the climb so difficult she wondered if she could make it. However, she found she could, and with relief, she went inside and set her purse on the table by the door.

"Mom?" Sam asked, and Kayla looked up to see Sam and Emma standing at the bottom of the staircase. "What happened?"

"James and I have parted ways," she explained as she wiped the tears off her cheeks.

Sam turned to Emma and placed a hand on her arm. "I hate to ask this, but can I talk to my mom alone for a minute?"

"Sure. No problem," Emma said and then headed back upstairs.

Kayla headed to the kitchen and Sam followed behind.

"So, it's over?" Sam asked, as if she had not heard Kayla correctly the first time. When Kayla nodded, she said, "What happened?"

"I found out a lot of things about James this morning, things that I can't allow myself to be associated with," she explained. "Not only was he in that biker gang that came into the diner, he also did time in prison."

"Okay?"

"Honey, there were a few other things, things that you don't need to know about. All you need to know is that we're done."

Sam shook her head. "I can't believe it," she said. Then she gave a firm nod to her head. "I'll talk to him when I go in to work next week."

"No, sweetie, you won't. I let him go."

Sam's jaw dropped. "Are you serious?" she asked. "You fired him?"

"Yes. Sam, he's a felon. I can't have that at the diner. Can you imagine if people found out? And trust me, they will."

Sam put her hand on her hip. "You're unbelievable."

"Excuse me, young lady?" Kayla asked, not caring for her daughter's tone.

"Mom, he has a shady past. Does it matter?"

"Yes, it does!"

"Why?" Sam demanded. "It's obvious he's a changed man. I like him…a lot." Tears ran down her cheeks. "I like having him around. He's been showing me things at work and teaching me things about life. And you go fire him? What's he going to do for work now? How's he going to pay his bills?"

Kayla sighed. Sam was not old enough to understand, and Kayla was not going to waste time trying to explain. "That's not my concern," she replied. "It just didn't work out."

Sam walked over, leaned against the kitchen counter, and crossed her arms over her chest. "You told me for a long time that God put James in your life, and it was something you prayed for. Now, you just up and dump him? He must feel really great." She rolled her eyes.

Kayla thought she would explode. "Okay, I will not take that attitude from you anymore. Stop it now."

Not only was she heartbroken, she felt sick. As much as she hated to admit it, much of what Sam was saying was true.

Her daughter snorted. "You taught me not to judge people, and yet, here you are doing it yourself. I can't believe you did this."

"Sam, listen. It's not the same."

Sam headed for the foyer. "I'm going back upstairs with Emma," she said without looking back.

Kayla sighed and took out a wine glass. A moment later, she filled it and then headed outside. Sitting under the umbrella at her patio table, her mind began to wander. Had she overreacted? Was his past that big of a deal? Maybe she had overreacted, but he had lied to her. No relationship could start with lies; it would only be a sign of things to come.

She took a sip of her wine, pulled out her phone, and called Susan.

Chapter Twenty-Three

It had been two days since James had last seen Kayla, but it felt like a lifetime. For the first time in quite a few years, he felt a heavy sadness. He wondered why God had allowed him to get this far with Kayla only to have her reject him. Though he wasn't sure why, he knew he must remain steadfast in prayer. He had looked for Kayla at church yesterday, but she had not been there. And neither had Susan. If his presence was going to keep them away, he would let Dave know that he would no longer be attending.

Since it was Monday morning, the tourists were out, but not in full force. As he sat on the park bench, he stared over at the diner across the street, missing everyone there. No longer would he enjoy the friendly banter as he worked with Betty and Susan, or when Deborah came in to take over for the evening shift. They had welcomed him into their family, and Kayla had kicked him right back out of it.

He saw her truck parked outside and his heart longed for her. How he wanted to go over, hold her and let her see inside his heart. But she had told him in no uncertain terms that it was over and to keep away. Even though it was killing him, he planned on honoring her wishes.

"You look like a lost dog," a woman said from behind him.

James turned, already knowing who it was. "Vicki," he said, looking up at her.

"I was going to call you later today to talk, but I think now works." When he nodded, she added, "Want to go grab a coffee?"

"I suppose," he replied and they walked across the park and over to Penny's Coffee Shop. The place was packed, but he found a table for two against a far wall.

"Let me go grab them," she said. "Save my seat."

While she was gone, James looked over the heads of the other customers and stared out onto Elm Street. He smiled at the memories of his first day in Hopes Crest. Him pulling up to the diner for the first time. Meeting Kayla as she stumbled over her words. Telling Sam about the dangers of smoking. Reversing the motorcycle out of the parking space with Kayla gripping his sides so hard he thought she would tear his skin.

"Here you go," Vicki said when she returned, setting a mug down in front of him.

He thanked her as she sat across from him. There were a million things he wanted to ask her, to tell her. But he wasn't sure where to begin. "Vicki, I need to ask you some things," he said.

She nodded and took a sip of her coffee as if unperturbed at his request.

He noticed she still wore the engagement ring he had bought her years ago.

"Go ahead."

He took a moment to gather his thoughts. "I don't know what you said exactly, but why did you feel it necessary to tell Kayla all those things about me?"

She set her mug down on the table and looked over at him. "Because she needs to know who you are. Let's be honest, you're both from two different worlds." She reached her hand across the table and grabbed his. "She can't take care of you like I can." A seductive smile crossed her lips.

He pulled his hand back as if she had burned him. "It was my business to tell her, not yours. You've caused more problems in my life than I needed."

She sneered. "Oh, excuse me, Mr. Righteous. I forgot you're now holier than anyone else."

"I'm not like that," he said, "I'm not proud of my past, but apparently you are. You're still proud of what you do."

"And what do I do, James? Tell me. What do I do that's so wrong?"

"You know she dumped me?" James asked, ignoring her question. "Two days ago, she straight up came over and broke up with me. Why would you want to do that to me?"

Again, she reached over and placed her hand on his. "Because I still love you. I need you and you know you need me."

He shook his head in frustration. "Look, we had something special," he said, "but that was a long time ago. I don't love you that way anymore."

"Why? Do you want me to go to church? Is that what it's going to take?"

"I'd love for you to go, but not for me, for you. There's a whole other world out there, Vicki. It's full of forgiveness, love, and most importantly peace."

She slapped her hand on the table with a boisterous laugh. "Oh, James, you really believe that, don't you? Tell me, what's changed so much in your life that you can swear to it? I bet you don't own a home. You work as a cook. Tell me, what's so great in your life?"

He smiled. "I can wake up every morning, look at myself in the mirror and not feel sick," he said. Vicki shook her head and wiped at her eyes, although he could tell that it embarrassed her. "You can have that, too, Vicki. Jesus is real, and His love is like nothing else you have ever experienced before."

She leaned over the table, her eyes fierce and her voice angry. "Don't you dare tell me that crap," she hissed. "He let a three-year-old girl get run over and die. And you act like he's your best friend. You're nuts." She stood up, glared down at him as she removed the engagement ring and set it on the table. "Goodbye, James."

As she turned to leave, he stood up and grabbed her arm. "I know the hurt you have. I had it, too. It landed me in prison and it's a huge burden to carry. That hurt has turned now to anger, and it's going to eat away at you for the rest of your life. It will torment you day and night." He looked at her, begging her with his eyes. "Just pray. He's there waiting."

She glared down at his hand, and he let go of her.

Glancing around, he saw that most people in the coffee shop were staring at him, some with their mouths hanging open.

"Sorry about your new princess," Vicki sneered. And then she was gone.

James returned to the table, picked up the ring and slid it into his pocket. He downed the last of his coffee, which had gone cold, and headed back outside. Even though the sun shone brightly in the sky, he felt cold inside. He closed his eyes and said a quick prayer for Vicki, hoping that her hurt and pain would leave and she would find the true source of peace. Then he prayed for Kayla and Sam and asked that, if it were still possible, that God would open the doors again. And if not, that He would watch over them.

When he finished with his prayer, he opened his eyes and walked over to the truck. A familiar laugh made him glance across the street. Kayla and Sam were walking to her truck, each with an arm around the other.

He smiled, glad they were getting along. Kayla had prayed for reconciliation with her daughter, and he was truly happy her prayers had been answered.

Now, he asked himself, would his be answered, as well?

***

As Kayla started up the truck, Sam said, "Hey, mom, look!" She pointed across the street.

Kayla followed her finger and her laughter died as she saw James getting into his truck. He looked so handsome, and yet so alone. Her heart went out to him. She wanted to run over to him and hold him. Yet, she could not bring herself to do that; he had lied about his past, and it was just too much to overcome.

"Can I say hi to him, please?" Sam begged.

Kayla bit at her lip. "I don't think that's a good idea," she said. "Besides, we have to meet Kyle at the house in a few."

"I'll make it real quick, I promise."

Finally, Kayla nodded and she watched as Sam ran across the road and gave James a hug. As the two talked, Kayla couldn't help but smile. She could not deny that James had been a big influence in Sam's life, and she was happy that Sam would listen to reason from someone, even if it wasn't Kayla.

A few minutes went by, and Sam came back.

"Okay, good news," Sam said as they got into the truck. "James said Kyle is good in his book and I have nothing to worry about."

Kayla smiled as she turned up the AC. "Is that so?" she asked. "Does my opinion not count?"

"Mom, it's not like that. James is a guy, and he knows how to spot the bad ones."

Kayla backed out of the space and put the truck in drive. "That's true," she assented. "He's good at that."

It was quiet for a moment, and as they turned onto the road that led to Lake Hope, Sam turned toward Kayla. "Do you ever wonder if God makes us go through things so we can learn a lesson out of it?"

Kayla smiled. "I do. Why do you ask?"

"Just wondering that maybe James went through stuff," she said. "I mean, if he didn't use to be a bad guy, it would be hard for him to spot bad guys, wouldn't it?"

"I suppose you could be right," Kayla agreed and then felt a funny feeling in her stomach. It wasn't a bad feeling but rather a tugging feeling. Shaking it off, she slowed the truck down as they came to the road leading to their home.

"Now," Kayla said, turning on her motherly voice, "Susan's going to be at the house, too, and we're going to be hanging out in the living room. No funny business out in the pool."

"Really?" Sam asked with a mocked tone of surprise. "We were totally planning on making out the whole time."

"Very funny!" Kayla said. Then she patted Sam on her leg. "But, all joking aside, I'm proud of you. You've come a long way over the last few months." She turned into the driveway and smiled when she saw both Susan's and Kyle's cars parked in front of the house.

"Thanks, mom," Sam said, a seriousness in her voice. "Thanks for trusting me and giving me another chance."

Kayla pulled the truck up next to Susan's sedan and turned off the ignition. She turned and leaned over to give her daughter a hug and a kiss on the cheek. "Of course. You're my daughter and I love you. We all deserve another chance."

Sam raised an eyebrow at Kayla, and Kayla felt her insides knot up. "You're right. Everyone does," she said.

Kayla felt guilt wash over her as she opened the door and stepped out. "Come on, let's make sure Susan isn't boring Kyle," she said, and they headed inside.

***

Kayla peeked through the blinds to see Kyle splashing water at Sam, but they were at least three feet apart.

"Kayla," Susan sighed, "You have to trust her. Besides, if he tries anything, I'll go out there and beat him up."

This made Kayla laugh and she allowed the blinds to fall back into place. It had been an hour since she and Sam had returned home, and after they had eaten, she had allowed Sam and Kyle to go swimming.

"You're right," Kayla sighed as she headed over to the couch. She plopped herself down with a leg doubled under her so she could face Susan.

Susan took a sip of her wine and then set it on the coffee table. "Okay, why were you not at church yesterday?" she demanded. "And don't give me that headache excuse. I was out of town so at least I had one."

Kayla shrugged. "I don't know," she replied. "I guess I didn't want to see him."

"Uh-huh. Because seeing him might make you reconsider what you did?"

Kayla laughed, wondering if Susan was drunk. "What I did? I'm not the one who lied."

"That's true, but do you think maybe he lied for a reason?"

"There's never a reason to lie," Kayla said stiffly. "Why are you defending him anyway?" It was bad enough James had betrayed her, why did her oldest and dearest friend have to also do so?

"Honey, you know I love you," Susan said, and Kayla felt an easiness slide over her. "We've been best friends since the day we met, but I think you shouldn't've done what you did."

Kayla stared at Susan. "Okay then, please, enlighten me," she said, not hiding her sarcasm.

Susan pulled back her hair back behind her ears. "He lied to you and held a lot back, right?" Kayla nodded. "Well, the way you reacted justified his fear of being rejected."

"His past makes a huge difference," Kayla tried to explain, although she felt she should not have to explain herself. "If I would've known before I started dating him, I probably would've stayed a mile away from him."

Susan shook her head. "But you judged him, Kayla. You threw him out on the street." She narrowed her eyes. "And don't lie to me, I know you still love him, don't you?"

Kayla nodded, though she hated to admit it. "I do still care for him, but I just can't get over the lying. And yes, I handled it horribly, I admit that, and perhaps I judged a little too harshly."

Susan scooted over, put her arms around Kayla and pulled her in for a hug. "I know you're hurting," she whispered, "but you eventually need to talk to him, air everything out."

Kayla nodded as she leaned back in the chair. "All right," she conceded with a heavy sigh. "I'll think about it."

"Good," Susan said, and they both turned when they heard Sam laugh loudly. "I'll go check on them."

Kayla nodded and then leaned back into the couch. It was true; she missed James, and maybe it might be worth talking to him, even if it was just to clear the air.

Chapter Twenty-Four

The last of the customers for the night left as Kayla smiled and held the door open for them. It was just past nine and she was exhausted. Over the past two weeks, she found herself coming to work more often. She waited tables, cleaned up the backroom numerous times, closed up for the night and then returned to open back up in the morning, all in an attempt to keep her mind off James and what had happened.

As she went to turn to lock the door, however, she paused and opened the door again.

"I know it's one minute past nine, but is there any chance we could grab a burger?" Pastor Dave asked, Maria smiling at his side.

"Only for you two," Kayla said as she moved aside to let them in. She locked the door behind them and then led them to a corner booth. "What are we drinking?"

"Coke for each of us," Maria said. "And we'll both have a bacon cheeseburger and cheese fries."

Kayla nodded and then headed over to the partition and smiled at Sam. "Dave and Maria are here," she told Sam. She relayed the order to her, filled two glasses with Coke and took them to the table.

"Here we go," she said, then placed the drinks in front of them. "So, are you two out on a date night?"

"Yeah, I wanted to watch the game but someone," —Dave motioned to Maria— "insisted we go out."

Maria laughed as she reached over and playfully slapped his arm. "Don't listen to him." She then smiled at Kayla. "Hey, would you mind pulling up a seat?"

Kayla nodded, grabbing a chair and brought it back to the table.

Dave took a drink from his glass and then turned his attention to Kayla. "We've missed you and Sam at church lately. It's been what? Two Sundays now?"

Kayla nodded, feeling bad for missing. "I've been under the weather."

"The kind of sickness one gets when they don't want to see anyone else?" Dave asked.

How would he know what her ailment was? But then she realized who would have told him. "Apparently James told you everything?" she said, unable to keep the anger from her voice.

Maria reached over and took Kayla's hand. "No. Well, we know you two are no longer seeing each other, but we don't know any of the details. And no, we are not asking."

"Thank you," Kayla replied with a sigh. "I mean, I do need to talk about it. And, I have to admit, I haven't really been sick."

"Oh, a lie?" Dave asked as he raised an eyebrow and leaned back in the booth's seat.

"Well, yes," she said, her face burning in embarrassment. "It's just a small one."

"I see," Dave said, his eyebrow still raised high. "So, on the scale of bad lies to not so bad, how do you think it ranks?"

Kayla looked at him in confusion. "I'm sorry for missing church. I didn't mean to lie, but I was afraid you two..." She stopped and swallowed hard, the realization hitting her. Just like James had done, she felt the need to lie to save herself from judgment. The guilt that hit her was hard, and Maria released her hand as Sam walked up.

"Wow, look at this," Maria exclaimed as Sam set the food down on the table. "Did you cook all of this?"

"I sure did!" Sam replied proudly. "James and Carl taught me a lot. I can cook just about everything." She gave them each a hug and then headed back into the kitchen.

"It's amazing what God has done with her over the last few months," Dave said, and then reached for a fry.

Kayla nodded. "It's wonderful. It's like a whole new daughter. And the great thing is that now my stress level is down." She pushed back the chair and stood. "Well, I'll leave you two alone."

Maria motioned her back to the chair. "Sorry, mouth was full," she said, then wiped her mouth with a napkin. "Stay for a minute and have a fry."

Kayla laughed and then reached over to take several fries from Maria's plate.

Dave set his drink down and turned toward her. "Kayla, I have a special guest coming this Sunday who's going to speak to the congregation. I'd really appreciate it if you and Sam can make it."

Kayla smiled. "Sure. I've been needing to talk to James...and get back to church. Sorry for missing."

"Nothing to apologize for. You know that," Dave assured her. "But I think both you and Sam will be blessed if you go."

Kayla nodded and then Maria changed the subject to other matters. As the three talked, Kayla began to think about James again. She had been too hard on him, and though he had lied, she had lied to. At the very least, she would talk to him Sunday and maybe try to listen to what he had to say.

Later, after finishing the cleanup and locking up the diner, Kayla and Sam headed home. Kayla found herself at the foot of her bed, knelt down in prayer. She had missed church, which was bad enough, but she also had been harboring feelings of anger. Praying for wisdom and an open heart, she asked God to forgive her. She also prayed that, after talking to James, he might forgive her, too.

***

James stood in the front row as the choir finished their final song. Taking a glance behind him, he saw Kayla and Sam sitting in their regular seats, and though they were not looking his way, he smiled, hoping somehow that smile would travel to Kayla.

Dave asked everyone to sit and the entire congregation did so with a soft rustle. "Today we are going to have a different type of service," he said as he stood behind the oak pulpit. "But before we start, I want to read something." He opened his Bible. "Turn to Romans, chapter eight, verse twenty-eight." He paused as he waited for everyone to find the passage and then read it aloud as many people read with him, including James. "'And we know that all things work together for good, to those who love God, to those who are called according to His purpose.'" He looked up at his audience. "Now with that in mind, I want you to listen carefully to our speaker. Peter?" He smiled at the man sitting next to James.

Peter stood and James handed him his cane before giving him an encouraging squeeze on his arm. The man looked down at James and smiled. "Thank you, brother," he said and then made his way up the short steps to behind the pulpit.

He looked around at the congregation; it was clear he was nervous, but when he spoke, his voice was strong. "It's a blessing to be here today," he said as he set his cane against the pulpit and placed his hands on either side of the top to steady himself. "So many times, we share verses, maybe even discuss them a little, but we never truly apply them to our lives. The verse Pastor Dave just read, that verse has great application to my life, and my hope today is that it will bless yours."

James smiled, knowing what was coming and feeling calm about it, though he could have been distressed.

"I've always been a Christian, well at least for as long as I can remember. Several years ago, life was going great—I had a child and another on the way. I had just gotten a job promotion and we were looking into buying a new house. God had blessed us beyond belief." He looked down at James. "Then one day while driving down a residential street, something horrible happened."

James bit at his lip but did not break the eye contact with Peter.

"I sneezed," Peter said in a quiet voice that would not have been heard if it was not for the microphone in front of his mouth. "A simple sneeze that all of us experience. But this sneeze distracted me long enough to not see a small child run out into the street. And then..." He paused and cleared his throat.

"It was too late by the time I realized what had happened. I had hit the little girl." Tears now ran down his face, but he did nothing to wipe them away. "I can't even impress upon you how horrible this can be. The knowledge that I took the life of a little girl, that I had taken her from her family."

Small sniffs could be heard behind James, and he glanced around and saw more than one person with a tissue dabbing at his or her eyes. Someone blew their nose loudly, but otherwise, the church was completely silent. Even the children seemed to sense the seriousness of this man's speech.

"I thought about running away, but I couldn't get myself to do that," Peter continued. "So, I waited there for the police. They took me down to the station, I gave my statement, and I was finally released when they determined it was an accident. However, though they did not find me guilty of a crime, I relived that moment every day for a very long time, and the guilt the police did not find in me plagued me every day. However, through prayer and the support of my family, I was able to come to terms with that guilt and was able to take the next step in my healing."

Maria walked up and placed a glass of water on the podium and gave him an encouraging smile. The congregation remained silent as he took a drink and set the glass on the small shelf in the back of the podium.

"It had been just a few months later when I heard a thumping at the door of my house. I didn't even think, the knock was so panicked. When I opened the door, a man stood there who I recognized, and he pushed me down before I even had the chance to speak. After he slammed the door behind him, he stared down at me with eyes so angry, I knew I was in trouble. That man beat me so badly, his words of anger and cursing filled the entryway as his fists pummeled me. I don't know how long the beating lasted, but the effects of it are permanent, and that's why I have to use a cane."

Whispers of shock filled the sanctuary. Several people shook their heads, clearly angry that this man had to endure such hatred. Others continued to dab at their eyes with their tissues.

"But you see, folks, all things work together. Not just good things. Not bad things. But *all* things. And in knowing that, God began to work in me, to show me something great in all of the hurt I caused and was caused to me. So today, I would like to introduce you to the man who crippled me. The man whose daughter I ran over and killed."

James stood and a collective gasp echoed through the room. Urgent whispers could be heard behind him as he walked up the steps to stand beside Peter. He glanced over to Maria and Dave, who both gave him a quick thumbs-up sign.

Peter pulled James in for a hug, patted him on the back and whispered, "They're all yours."

"Thank you, brother," James whispered back.

As Peter made his way back to his seat, James turned to the congregation and saw a mixture of emotions on the people's faces. A few glared, some stared at him wide-eyed, but most smiled, and he cleared his throat.

"All things do work together, and I'm going to tell you how," he said, and then began to tell his story.

Chapter Twenty-Five

Kayla grabbed another tissue and dabbed at her eyes. Peter's story was heartbreaking enough; the pain the man went through for what he did had to have been horrendous. However, as she watched James take the pulpit, she wondered if the few tissues she had in her purse would be enough.

"All it took was a moment of distraction for Peter and a moment of me working on my bike and then my daughter was gone. I remember running down the driveway and seeing…my little girl lifeless," James said, his hands gripping the podium. To see him like this broke her heart, and Kayla wished she could comfort him.

"I never believed in God but at that moment, I asked him to save my daughter. But He didn't. And when she was pronounced dead not even an hour later, rage filled my heart and mind." James shook his head and then continued.

"That day I went to Peter's house, I was so filled with rage, I could barely make out the front door, my vision was so blind," James said. "I had never felt such anger, such hatred, as I did that day. Losing my daughter sent me down a path I never knew existed, but to have the man who was responsible for her death to get off scot-free was more than I could handle. In my mind, I wanted him to pay."

Kayla wondered at his ability to speak of what had happened with such calmness. This man he spoke of was not the James she knew.

"As Peter said, I beat him to within an inch of his life, and if the police had not come when they had, I might have killed him, that was how mad I was, how angry. I hated him. He had ruined my life, had taken something from me that I held dear, and I wanted him to pay."

Sam moved in closer to Kayla, and Kayla put her arm around her and pulled her in. She could hear her sniffle, and Mrs. Wagner handed her a tissue. Sam took it and thanked the woman with a nod.

"I was charged with attempted murder but pleaded guilty to felonious assault and sent to prison. Even after the first two months of being locked up, I still raged in my cell. So, as I rotted away in that damp room, my heart was rotting even faster. However, I also realized that I had nothing more to live for. My daughter was gone, so what was there?

"Then, two months after my sentencing, I was told I had a visitor. Not many people had been by in those two months, so you can imagine my surprise when it was Peter in that visiting room. The man who killed my daughter, the man I hurt, was there." James wiped at his eyes and Kayla wished she could run up and hold him.

"He tells me that he's there to tell me about Jesus," James continued. "I remember rolling my eyes at him, wondering why this man who had murdered could be outside and alive enjoying his life, while my daughter was buried beneath the cold ground. Then he told me that he forgave me for what I did to him and asked would I be willing to forgive him as well. At first I thought he was joking."

He glanced down at the front row and Peter shouted, "It's true!" and then James returned to his testimony.

"I didn't want to hear what he had to say, so I told him in no uncertain terms to go away, that he was a murderer, and that he didn't deserve forgiveness and that this God he thought he worshiped could never forgive him."

James cleared his throat, picked up the glass of water and took a drink. "But the man came back. Each time he came, I rejected him, told him to go away. All I wanted was for him to stop coming to see me, so after a whole year of this man repeating the same things, I figured I would let him say what he needed to say. I couldn't have cared less; if it made him feel better, then so be it. I could continue to hate him either way.

"However, what I learned was about a man who sneezed, and how that simple act had changed his life forever, his own guilt plaguing him and causing distress in his own family. How he had learned to forgive himself for what part he had played in my daughter's death and how God had forgiven him despite how tragic it was. But the most important thing I learned was how he forgave the man who had crippled him, who had taken away his ability to play ball with his new son. How he had been unable to return to his job because he was not physically capable of performing it. How his life had been turned upside down. Yet, he forgave me.

"Peter learned that an angry biker who hated the world had been running on hate his whole life, a hate that had sent him over the edge, and sent him to kill the man who took the only light he had in his life."

Kayla was weeping, and Sam held her tighter. How she had judged him, casting him to the side like he had the plague. He was a good man, and she had held his 'lie' over his head. Had she not lied, as well? How many times in her life, as Dave and Maria pointed out a few nights ago, had she told untruths, even those she considered small such as reasons for missing church.

"Once Peter shared his story and learned about me, he visited me regularly. Then one day, he came to see me."

Peter made his way back up front to stand beside James as James spoke.

"I had been attending Bible studies with other inmates even as Peter continued to drop by to see me. On that particular day when Peter came to see me, I shared something with him that I never thought I would ever have shared with anyone, because it was not something I had ever considered in my hate-filled life. I told him I had become saved, for which he was very happy."

Peter patted James on the back. "I was, it's true," he said with a smile.

"But I also told him that I forgave him for what had happened that fateful day on the street in front of my house and, more importantly, that God had forgiven us both."

179

The two men hugged and the entire congregation was on its feet in a round of applause that rattled the windows as people shouted, "Praise the Lord!" and "Praise God!".

As James took the mic again, the applause died down and everyone retook their seats. There was not a dry eye in the house.

"As Dave stated earlier, 'all things work together'. A simple sneeze led to the death of my daughter, who I miss still. But that led to me hurting Peter, which led to me going to prison. However, that led to Peter visiting me, which led to two men who are now good friends standing before you together today to share our testimonies.

"So, the next time something good, or even bad, happens, just remember, God is in control and it's all working together for the good of God."

The applause that followed was greater than the previous as Dave made his way back to the pulpit. It took several attempts, but Dave calmed the congregation.

Sam shook in Kayla's arm and Kayla looked down. Her daughter wept harder than Kayla had seen her weep in a very long time, and Kayla held her close.

"Molly, do you want to come up here?" Dave asked from the pulpit. Kayla had not seen that Molly and Emma remained standing a few rows from her and Sam.

"No, that's okay. Can everyone hear me?" Several people said yes, and Molly pulled her daughter in beside her. "Me and Emma have never been to church; I never thought of it as a thing for me. But meeting James a couple of months ago, he told me to give it a try. Well, it wasn't as lame as I had heard." A few people laughed and she continued. "The point is, the message today of all things working together? It's true. You see, if James hadn't been saved and hadn't moved here, I would never have been bothered going to church. And me and Emma, well, we wouldn't have asked Jesus into our hearts last week."

Kayla could not stop the tears that streamed down her face, and she did not even try. She needed the comfort of her tears, for they were tears of joy and not of sadness or anger.

"Mom?" Sam said, her voice shaky as she continued to weep.

Kayla brushed at her daughter's cheeks. "Yes?"

"God finally answered my prayers," she said in a small voice. "I understand now why He took dad." She leaned over and sobbed into Kayla's chest and Kayla hugged her tightly. "It's all part of His plan," Sam said, her choked voice muffled by Kayla's coat. "Things we don't know sometimes. But we have to trust Him in all things, don't we?"

"We do, sweetie. We sure do."

***

Kayla sat in her truck and rubbed her stinging eyes. Church had let out almost an hour ago, and Sam had gone with Susan back to the house so Kayla could wait for James. There was so much to apologize for, so much she needed to ask forgiveness for, and she was not going to wait for another day to make her apologies.

She smiled when the front door of the church opened and James walked out. She had seen the man who had spoken, Peter, leave ten minutes earlier, and though she wanted to walk up to him and let him know how much his story had touched her, she knew he had already been inundated with people's words already. Instead, she sent up a prayer for him, that he would continue to be such a beacon of light to so many people.

James made his way across the parking lot to his motorcycle, which was parked a few spaces from her truck.

She got out of the truck and walked toward him, her steps slow as she built up her courage.

He stopped in his tracks, the familiar smile lit up on his face. "Kayla?"

"I-I need to talk to you," Kayla said, her heart pounding against her chest.

"Of course," he said. "Please, tell me whatever you'd like."

Although his words were kind, they stung at Kayla's heart. She knew it was not his intention, but her guilt was so strong, she could not help it.

"I want to apologize for the way I treated you," she said as she looked down at the ground in shame. "There was no excuse for how I behaved. I judged you and then cast you aside—the very thing I feared people would do to me if they knew the things I've done."

He nodded, not saying anything. It was as if he knew she needed to get out what she had to say.

"You're a good man, and my own jealousy, insecurities, and whatever else I have going on, I threw aside the very thing I had prayed for. You see, you've been the answer to my prayers." She walked up to stand directly in front of him and gazed up into his eyes. "You helped Sam start talking to me. You showed me a part of me that I didn't know existed and led me to deal with a part of me that needed to be dealt with. And the way I showed my thanks was...terrible." She took his hand in hers. "I hope you can forgive me."

He took another step forward, though it was not a wide space to cover. "I forgive you," he said in a soft voice. "Thank you for letting me into your life. I'm sorry I lied to you or played coy along the way. I was so scared that I would lose you that it caused me to spiral down a path of wondering 'what if?'." He sighed. "I believed that God brought us together, and then I forgot about Him along the way. I guess I kind of figured that I could handle it myself, and that's when it all went wrong. I'm sorry, Kayla. I hope you can forgive me, too."

She gazed up into his eyes and felt a warmness wash over her. She nodded and he pulled her into his arms into a tight embrace. A light breeze blew as they stood there together in the silent and empty church parking lot.

When the embrace ended, Kayla looked into his eyes once more. "There's something else," she said. "I wanted to tell you before I messed everything up." He gave her an expectant look but said nothing. "I never thought it was possible so quickly, but I fell in love with you," she said, her heart racing. "If you're still interested, I still want to be your girlfriend." Then, summoning a final bit of courage, she whispered, "I love you."

James was staring at her with what she hoped was love in his eyes. "I felt the same, and still do," he replied. "I want to put all this behind us. I love you, Kayla."

Kayla thought her heart would soar to the sky above. She put her arms around his neck and pulled him to her, their lips meeting in a deep kiss that held passion, forgiveness, and most importantly, love.

When the kiss broke, she took his hands in hers again. "I learned today that all things work together," she said with a smile that she hoped would express how much she truly did love him. "Thank you for being you. I love you."

"I love you, too."

Whether it was a minute or an hour, Kayla did not know, but they stood there in the parking lot, James holding her tightly as Kayla listened to his heartbeat in her ear, its rhythm matching her own. There were things she had done wrong, and maybe a few he could have done better, but it did not matter now. Those things were in the past, and now, God willing, there was a future ahead for them both.

Together.

***

Kayla entered her home, with James by her side. Hand in hand they walked into the kitchen where Susan sat waiting on a stool next to the island, a cup of coffee in her hand.

Susan turned and smiled when she heard them. "Hey, you two," she called out, "you're just in time. Lunch's almost ready." She walked over to James and gave him a big hug. "It's good to see you again, handsome." She squeezed his bicep.

Kayla laughed and playfully slapped her hand away. Then Kayla put her arms around her best friend and hugged her. "Love you," she said in Susan's ear.

"Love you," Susan replied. "I'm glad to see you guys back together." A moment later the hug broke and Susan returned to the stove to stir whatever it was she was cooking.

The sound of footsteps greeted Kayla's ear and she turned to see Sam standing in the doorway, her eyes puffy and red.

"Hey, big guy," Sam said, her nose stuffy, "you back?"

"I am," James replied with a wide smile. "Do you want me around?"

Sam stood staring at him for a moment and then ran to him. He pulled her into his arms and the two embraced tightly.

Kayla held her hand to her chest, surprised by her daughter's actions, but pleased beyond belief. A moment passed and the hug broke.

"Tomorrow, Kyle's coming over to watch a movie with me," Sam said as she went to the counter and grabbed a cut carrot from the vegetable tray Susan had set out. "You're going to give him the talk." She made a fist and pushed it into her other hand in a menacing manner, making everyone laugh.

"You bet I will," James said with a seriousness to his face. Then he broke out with a smile.

Kayla helped Susan set the table and a few minutes later, the places were set and the food was ready.

"I don't know about you," Susan said as she started to pull out the chair at the head of the table, "but I'm starving."

Sam reached over and grabbed the chair from Susan. "Aunt Susan, I'm sorry, but you can't sit there." Susan stared at Sam but then nodded as she sat in another chair. Then Sam went over to James, took his hand and led him to the table. "This chair is for James."

Kayla had thought she had cried as many tears as she could have that day, but she found that she still had some left, for they spilled over her lashes and ran down her cheeks as James hugged Sam again and gingerly sat in what once been Brandon's seat as if, at any moment, it might fall under him.

However, the chair remained strong and soon, everyone was seated. James led them all in a prayer of thanksgiving and when everyone said, "Amen," they filled their plates with food, laughed, talked, ate, and simply enjoyed the company of those around them.

Kayla could not help but smile as James passed a dish to her, and she realized that all her prayers had been answered. Granted, they had not been answered in the way she had expected, but that was the funny thing about life; it could be heartbreaking one moment and full of love the next.

Who would have imagined an ex-con who lost his child, a teenage daughter that was hell-bent on destruction, and a widowed mother who had wanted a new start in life, that they would all come together sitting at the same table? Yet somehow it had all worked out by the grace of God with one thing that held it all in place.

Love.

Epilogue

Kayla laughed. Sam stood before her, a hand on her hip and her head tilted to the side with a serious look on her face.

"Now, Aunt Susan and I are going to be right behind you," Sam said firmly in a motherly tone Kayla recognized all too easily because she had used it often enough on her daughter. "So, I want you both to be on your best behavior."

Kayla laughed even harder but shook her head nonetheless. "We promise," she replied between gasps.

"Are you sure you girls don't want to go buy a tent?" James asked, patting the tied camping gear on his bike. "Cabins are for wimps."

"No way," Sam said firmly. "You can suffer alone; we girls need our electricity and running water."

"Suit yourself."

Kayla laughed and turned back to Sam. "Now, if you're done telling us all what to do, can we go?"

"You bet," Sam said and then ran back to the SUV.

The four of them—Kayla, Sam, James, and Susan—were on their way for a few days of R&R for the weekend. They had rented a cabin for the girls in a picturesque area, and James was going to camp out in his tent, and Kayla could not wait. It would be the perfect weekend; time to spend with her daughter and best friend with a bit of boyfriend alone-time mingled in. It could not get any better than that.

"You know," James said as he handed Kayla her helmet, "you're traveling on a motorcycle for an entire weekend. What's next on your daredevil list?"

"Monster truck rallies," she replied without missing a beat and then gave him a quick wink, which made him chuckle. They both smiled at one another, something they had become fond of doing these days whenever they looked at each other.

"Hey!" Sam yelled from the front seat of the SUV. "Save that mushy stuff for later and let's get going."

Kayla laughed again and slipped the helmet over her head. Then she crawled onto the back of the motorcycle behind James.

He fired it up and they drove off, leaving behind the neighborhood before picking up speed when they reached the open road. The scenery flew by as they wound their way through the winding mountain roads. Snow was already collecting on the mountain peaks and they would soon be covered in a thick white blanket once winter arrived.

She smiled as she thought of the coming New Year and what it would bring. However, to Kayla, it was already a new year, a time for celebration for all God had done in their lives. And as they continued their ride, she tightened her grip on the man she loved, knowing their celebration had only just begun.

Author's Note

Romans 8:28 - And we know that all things work together for good, to those who love God, to those who are called according to His purpose.

I hope this story has touched your heart and that you have loved the characters as much as I have loved writing about them. God never promised that we would not suffer, nor did He promise that we would not have troubles in our lives. However, He did promise that, no matter what happens, good and bad, it is all for His good and for His glory. So, with that promise, know that whatever you might be going through in your life, He is there, always present. And though we may not see the results, He is forever in control.

May God bless you and keep you,

Laura

Made in the USA
Monee, IL
12 September 2021

77883444R00111